Born in 1912, **Anthony Buckeridge** was sent to boarding school in Sussex at the age of eight. He went on to university before working as a tutor in a preparatory school and later became a fireman during the Second World War. Buckeridge was the first writer to use prep schools as a setting for his stories and, as such, is the creator of the infamous Jennings. He has written twenty-five 'Jennings' titles in total, which have sold over six million books worldwide, and he was awarded an OBE in the 2003 New Years Honours List. Anthony Buckeridge lives in Sussex with his wife, Eileen.

BY THE SAME AUTHOR
ALL PUBLISHED BY HOUSE OF STRATUS

Jennings
Follows a Clue

HOUSE OF
STRATUS

This edition published in 2001 by House of Stratus, an imprint of
House of Stratus Ltd, Thirsk Industrial Park, York Road, Thirsk,
North Yorkshire, YO7 3BX, UK.
Also at: House of Stratus Inc., 2 Neptune Road, Poughkeepsie, NY 12601, USA.

www.houseofstratus.com

Typeset by House of Stratus, printed and bound by Short Run Press Limited.

A catalogue record for this book is available from the British Library
and the Library of Congress.

ISBN 0-7551-1366-7

The Jennings books of Anthony Buckeridge span the years 1950–2000. Many social changes occurred during this time including the adoption of decimal currency in 1971 to replace that of pounds, shillings and pence. This edition contains all the original writings of Anthony Buckeridge and has not been altered or changed in any way.

Contents

1

Mr Carter Reads Aloud

During the first half of the Easter term the weather chose Wednesdays when it wanted to be unpleasant. This was because Wednesday was a half-holiday, and for two weeks in succession the grumbling February sky had decided that the half-holiday should be a wet one. Outside, the rain pattered down and the trees dripped, and big puddles on the rugger pitch grew into little lakes. Inside, the seventy-nine boys of Linbury Court Preparatory School refused to be depressed, and settled down for another afternoon of indoor activity.

In the common room, the noise made by a group of twenty boys suggested that to be active indoors meant creating enough sound to raise the roof and shake the foundations of the building. Odd pieces of wood were being hammered and chiselled into model yachts; biscuit tins were being beaten into gleaming aeroplane wings; the stage-manager of the puppet theatre, busily rehearsing the sound effects for the next production, was imitating rolls of thunder with a tea-tray and a gong stick; while his assistant smote an empty box with a riding crop, in the vain hope that it sounded like rifle fire. Near the rattling windows, members of the wireless club with home-made sets tuned to rival stations, relayed grand opera, military bands and talks in Norwegian all at the same time.

1

Other boys were playing an improvised game of hockey, knocking a boxing glove round the room with cricket stumps and making the floor vibrate with their perpetual commotion.

In the middle of the room where the uproar was most deafening, Jennings and Darbishire, with their fingers pressed to their ears, were enjoying a quiet game of chess.

Jennings was the taller of the two, a friendly-looking boy of ten with an untidy fringe of brown hair and a wide-awake look in his eyes. His opponent was fair and curly; he had a pink and white complexion and pale blue eyes that gazed beadily at the chessboard through large spectacles. Doubtfully he moved a pawn, hesitated, changed his mind and shifted his king to the next square. Jennings unplugged his ears and shaped his hands into a megaphone.

"You can't do that, Darbishire," he shouted at the top of his voice. "You've made a bish and put yourself in check."

A resounding crash of thunder from the puppet theatre drowned his words and Darbishire cupped one hand to his ear, while his raised eyebrows signalled for the message to be repeated.

"I said," Jennings began again, but at that moment the boxing glove landed in the middle of the chessboard, scattering the pieces over a wide area.

Darbishire grovelled about on his hands and knees to retrieve them, while Jennings relieved his feelings by hurling the boxing glove at Bromwich major who had come to claim it.

"You ozard oik, Bromo," Jennings shouted. "Can't you see Darbi and I are playing an important game? This is supposed to be the finals of the Form III chess championship."

The words had little effect on Bromwich major as he was unable to hear them, but the boxing glove, catching him squarely on the nose, made Jennings' meaning quite clear, and the hockey players retired to the far end of the room.

Darbishire replaced the chessmen, and Jennings tried again to explain that it was against the rules to move into check; but Binns minor was hammering a biscuit tin with his house-shoe and the words were carried away in the stream of sound.

"What did you say?" Darbishire mouthed back at him politely, though his voice was inaudible.

Jennings took a deep breath and replied with the full force of his lungs, but at that moment the door opened and the Headmaster appeared.

Instantly the noise of the room was stilled; loudspeakers were switched off, the thunder died away, hammers paused in mid-beat and the hockey players changed to statues wearing fixed, innocent smiles. The Headmaster looked round, satisfied at the sight of so much indoor activity. He had no objection to noise in the common room provided that it ceased whenever he entered.

But it had not ceased entirely; Jennings, with his back to the door and his fingers still pressed to his ears, was unaware of the Headmaster's arrival, and carried on at full volume.

"I said you can't move there, Darbi," he shouted. "And that's the second time you've bished up the rules. You've got no more idea how to play chess than a suet pudding..."

He stopped abruptly, aware that his voice alone was shattering the unnatural silence and that Darbishire, round-eyed with apprehension, was blinking out an agonised signal of warning.

Jennings looked up; the Headmaster was standing just behind him.

"I am at a loss to understand, Jennings," the Headmaster began, "why you should find it necessary to make more noise than everyone else in the room put together. I should be the first to agree that the making of model aeroplanes and wireless sets cannot be done in complete silence; and yet, when I enter the room, these noises are hushed, and the only sound which affronts my ears is your voice, upraised in brawling discord at an opponent who is seated less than two feet away from you."

"Yes, sir," said Jennings.

"Darbishire is not deaf so far as I am aware, though undoubtedly he soon will be if you continue to bellow down his ear in that ungentlemanly fashion."

"Yes, sir," said Jennings. It was useless to explain that, until the Headmaster's entry, the chessboard had been an oasis of silence in a desert of tumult, for Mr Pemberton-Oakes had passed on to the next stage of his lecture.

"Chess," he continued, "is a game that demands quiet, thoughtful concentration. And as you appear to be unable to play without disturbing everyone else in the room, you will cease to enjoy the amenities of the common room for the remainder of the day."

"I shall cease to enjoy what, sir?" asked Jennings, unable by this time to feel like enjoying anything.

"You will not be allowed to use the common room," translated the Headmaster.

"Yes, sir," said Jennings. It was rather unfair, he thought, that the first remark which he had been able to make Darbishire hear for twenty minutes should be followed by this unfortunate punishment. He'd like to see the Headmaster indulging in quiet, thoughtful concentration with Binns minor banging a biscuit tin half an inch from his ear. However, one does not argue with Headmasters. Jennings walked sadly from the room, leaving Darbishire still wondering what it was that his friend had been trying to tell him.

It was still raining hard and Jennings made for the tuck-box room, as he felt that only ginger biscuits and milk chocolate would cheer his drooping spirits. As he entered the door, he noticed with shocked surprise that two boys were trying to open his tuck-box.

"Hey, Venables," he called, as the elder of the two looked up on his approach. "Who gave you permish to go to my tuck-box?"

"It's all right, Jennings," replied Venables, a tall boy of eleven, "we shan't touch anything. You see, Atkinson and I are being cat burglars."

"Yes, it's super rare," explained Atkinson eagerly. "We're the terror of half the capitals of Europe, and we go about barking defiance at the police of every continent." He was a thin, rather nervous-looking boy of ten who looked incapable of defying anything for very long. "Your tuck-box is a fireproof safe with a super decent combination lock that we've got to pick, so that we can steal the secret plans."

"What secret plans?"

"Any ones'll do. All safes have secret plans. You can be the detective who's after us, if you like."

"Coo – yes," said Jennings, cheering up at once. "I'll be Chief Detective-Inspector Jennings. Look out, I've got a gun!" He levelled a broken pencil at them and hissed a series of sharp clicking noises through his back teeth.

The thieves abandoned the safe, leapt through an imaginary window and scaled an imaginary drainpipe with the detective in pursuit. An exciting roof-top chase followed, as the burglars scrambled over tuck-boxes and took cover behind boot-lockers. All three were heavily armed, and the tuck-box room rang with a fusillade of exploding shots as the three boys clicked and hissed their way from corner to corner.

"Dacka-dacka-dacka-dacka!" Jennings discarded his automatic and conjured up a machine-gun out of thin air. "Come on, Atkinson! I got you that time," he called.

"No you didn't then," objected the safe-breaker, "because my pullover is a bullet-proof waistcoat."

"Ah, but I got you in the leg," countered the chief detective-inspector.

"But it's not fair to shoot below the belt, is it, Venables?" Atkinson appealed to his partner, but Venables had gone to earth behind the farthest boot-lockers and was not going to betray his whereabouts.

"You're under arrest, Atkinson," Jennings announced.

"I don't think it's fair," protested the terror of half Europe. "I wasn't ready that last time, and below the belt doesn't count anyway."

"Well, I like that," retorted the detective. "I gave you five bursts of machine-gun fire at point-blank range, so you can't grumble. And in any case, you're standing on Paterson's tuck-box and that's an unexploded minefield, so that proves it."

Atkinson, still complaining bitterly about the injustice of the police, was led away and handcuffed to the doorknob by his tie, and Jennings went in search of the second arch-criminal. Again his machine-gun spluttered viciously.

"Come on, Venables," he called. "I can see you lying there. Get up and come out – you're dead!"

"No, I'm not," replied Venables. "I dodged."

"You couldn't have dodged all of them. I gave you a ten-second burst."

"Well, anyway," argued the corpse, logically, "if I'm dead I can't get up and come out."

Venables' protests were ignored and he, too, was led away and secured to the doorknob.

"Now," said Jennings, "you've got to stay there while I round up the rest of the gang. And if you try to run away I shall shoot you within an inch of your life."

The chief detective-inspector skipped nimbly into his autogyro and, waving his arms round his head like a propeller, raced off down the corridor with his engine roaring, and his ammunition spattering at stray foes lurking behind orderly rows of rugger vests.

"Eee-ow-ow! Eee-ow-ow! Dacka-dacka-dacka-dacka... Whomp!"

It does not often happen that a schoolmaster in his early thirties turns a corner and collides with an autogyro. Mr Carter winced, for Jennings' head was hard and it caught him on the third button of his waistcoat.

Jennings recoiled and sat down; then, gabbling profuse apologies, he jumped up and retrieved Mr Carter's pipe from behind a radiator, where the force of the collision had thrown it.

"Oh, sir, I'm terribly sorry, sir, honestly I am, sir. I didn't mean to bump into you, sir."

Mr Carter breathed heavily while he regained his composure.

"Why on earth can't you go along a corridor like a civilised human being? Do you find it difficult to walk without waving your arms and legs like a windmill?"

"No, sir."

"This is the third time this week," said Mr Carter, "that your flailing tentacles have nearly knocked me down. On Monday, you explained that you were practising imaginary leg-breaks. Yesterday, you were a paddle-steamer on the Congo. What are you this time – a revolving door or a Catherine wheel?"

"Neither, sir. I'm an autogyro."

"I see. And what are you doing down here?" Mr Carter asked. "I thought that you and Darbishire were going to settle down quietly and play off the final of the Form III chess tournament?"

"Yes, we were, sir," Jennings explained, "but the Head came in and said that our chess was disturbing the people who were trying to hammer."

Mr Carter glanced down the corridor to the open door of the tuck-box room.

"And why," he wanted to know, "are Venables and Atkinson wearing their ties round their wrists? Is it a new fashion?"

"No, sir, they're handcuffed," Jennings explained. "You see, they're a gang of international safe-breakers, and they're armed to the teeth with guns and bombs and things, and I'm a famous detective in an autogyro, and we keep shooting each other, sir."

Mr Carter sighed. "And that, I suppose, is your idea of how a detective goes to work?"

"Well, perhaps not in real life, but that's how they do it in books, isn't it, sir?"

"No," said Mr Carter, "not in the best books. Haven't you ever read *The Adventures of Sherlock Holmes*?"

"I'm afraid I haven't, sir."

"Well, Sherlock Holmes trained himself to observe clues that other people had overlooked, or dismissed as being unimportant," Mr Carter said. "Then he'd fix his mind on the problem he was trying to solve until he had fitted all the clues together, like pieces of a jig-saw puzzle. No autogyros, no machine-guns, just intelligent deduction."

"Sounds rather a dull way of doing it, sir."

"Dull!" Mr Carter was shocked He looked out of the window at the falling rain. There was no chance of letting the boys out on to the playing field to work off their surplus energy; on the other hand, the tuck-box room was not the place for roof-top chases and hairbreadth escapes.

"Go and untie Venables and Atkinson," he said, "and then all three of you come along to my room, and I'll read to you."

"Coo, will you really, sir! Super thanks, sir! Something decent, sir?"

"I will read you *The Adventures of Sherlock Holmes*," said Mr Carter, "and then, perhaps, you will see that using your brain is a better way of playing at detectives than stampeding about the corridor like a herd of wildebeeste crossing the veldt."

Five minutes later Jennings, Venables and Atkinson were seated on the rug in front of the fire in Mr Carter's study. It was a pleasant, comfortable room. There were thick rugs and large armchairs, and the walls were lined with books wearing coloured dust-jackets. In one corner stood a radiogram with cases of gramophone records stacked beside it; and looking oddly out of place amongst the modern pictures on the walls, was a fifteen-year-old photograph of a university rugger team, in which a younger, thinner Mr Carter stood self-consciously in the back row.

Mr Carter settled himself comfortably in an armchair and read aloud; and as the plot unfolded, Jennings' lively imagination was soon at work, adapting the story so that it fitted in with his own surroundings. Gradually, the housemaster's study merged into Sherlock Holmes' flat in Baker Street. The rain beating on the window-panes became a thick London fog; a gas mantle glimmered in the electric reading lamp, and the dust-jackets shrouded the great detective's case-books.

Very soon, Jennings and Sherlock Holmes became, in imagination, the same person. The MA gown on the back of the door was his dressing-gown, the raincoat and brown felt hat were his cape and deerstalker. Casually, Jennings took a broken pencil from his pocket and held it between his teeth; but it was no ordinary pencil – it was an old briar pipe with a stem which was curved like a saxophone.

Once or twice, Mr Carter raised his eyes from the page and noted that the thoughts of the great detective were being faithfully mirrored in Jennings' features. When Sherlock Holmes was keen and alert, so was Jennings; when the detective sat back with his fingertips pressed together and surveyed his client through half-closed lids, Jennings leant against the coal scuttle and screwed up his eyes as though blinded by a beam of light. There was no doubt about it; half an hour of *The Adventures of Sherlock Holmes* had convinced Jennings that there was more in being a detective than blazing away with imaginary machine-guns.

"Coo – thank you, sir, that was supersonic!" said Venables, as Mr Carter put the book down.

"Yes, thanks for reading. It was wizard decent of you, sir," added Atkinson. But Jennings' brain was buzzing too busily to allow him to utter more than a polite "Thank you, sir," as he walked out of the room.

"Come on, Jennings, let's go and do our stamp albums," suggested Venables, "and we can pretend Atkinson's a crook who's pinched a stamp that's so rare it's extinct, and we have to chase him to get it back."

Jennings shook his head. Chasing about was all very well as a game, but a real detective's world was made up of something more subtle – clues, theories, motives, observations and deduction.

Venables and Atkinson raced down the stairs from Mr Carter's room, but Jennings followed slowly, deep in thought. It should not be too difficult to become a detective, once you knew how it was done. He sat down on the bottom stair, determined to see whether clear reasoning and minute observation would deduce any interesting facts from a wastepaper basket and a noticeboard, which were the only objects insight. With his pencil gripped between his teeth and the tips of his fingers pressed together, he was surveying them through half-closed lids, when his mood was shattered by the sudden appearance of Darbishire.

"Golly," said Darbishire, "have you gone bats? You look like the ghost of Hamlet's father."

Jennings came out of his trance and got up.

"I've been looking for you everywhere," Darbishire went on. "I thought you'd go to the games room when the Head turfed you out for kicking up a hoo-hah, and I went and bagged the ping-pong table, and then you never turned up."

"I've been busy," Jennings replied. "Mr Carter's been reading to us. It was super! He just sits back and looks at you through half-closed eyelids, and deduces things like, say, for instance, you bowl left-handed off-breaks, or you had measles when you were young."

"What!" exclaimed Darbishire in surprise. "Mr Carter says that?"

"No, Sherlock Holmes does. You see," he went on hurriedly, "he said he'd read to us because I beetled round a corner in top gear and doynged into him."

"Who, Sherlock Holmes?"

"No, Mr Carter. Why don't you listen? He's been reading to us about Sherlock Holmes. For instance, he can tell, just by looking at you, that your uncle's got a wooden leg. You'd be surprised."

"Yes, I would if he told me that," Darbishire replied solemnly, "because my uncle hasn't got a wooden leg, and my father says that – "

"Don't be so dim, Darbishire; you don't have to have an uncle with a wooden leg."

"Well, why should Sherlock Holmes say that I had?"

"That's just an example of deduction," Jennings explained. "He can deduce things that you don't know about."

"Oh, I see!" Darbishire pondered this for a moment; then he went on: "Of course, I *have* got an uncle in Australia whom I've never seen. He might have got a wooden leg, mightn't he?"

"Well, there you are then!" said Jennings triumphantly. "That proves it. And when you gasp with astonishment he just says – 'Elementary, my dear Watson! You know my methods.'"

An electric bell shrilled out its message, and together they went to the washroom to get ready for tea.

"Gosh," said Jennings longingly, drying his hands on the legs of his trousers. "Gosh, I wish I was a famous detective."

"Fat lot of good it is wanting to be a detective at boarding school," retorted the practical Darbishire. "It's all very well for Sherlock Holmes and people – things happen to them, but nothing ever happens to us."

"I know, it's a swizz. You never get any decent murders and things at school. Still, we could have a bash at deducing things by looking at people, couldn't we?"

"Well, what can you tell by looking at me?" asked Darbishire, as he splashed his curly hair with water and combed vigorously.

Jennings narrowed his eyes and stared at his friend intently.

"H'm," he said at length. "I should say you'd had an egg for breakfast this morning."

"Gosh, yes, you're right," cried Darbishire. "Super decent deduction! How on earth did you know?"

"You've got traces of egg on your tie which are faintly invisible except to the trained eye," Jennings explained. "Of course, ordinary people might not be able to spot them, but it's quite easy if you're any good at observation."

Darbishire contorted the muscles of his jaw and squinted down his nose, trying to see the knot of his tie.

"You don't have to make a face like a bullfrog," his friend pointed out. "Look, there's a hunk of egg stain lower down – just between those two ink spots."

"Golly, so there is. I think that's wizard!"

Darbishire was thrilled at the possibilities that lay open to the trained mind. "And even if, supposing, they weren't egg stains; supposing they were rare chemicals, say – of course they're not, but they might easily be – and just supposing they were, you'd be able to tell that I was a – " He broke off as his flight of fancy suddenly made a forced landing. "Ah, but we *all* had eggs for breakfast this morning," he went on, as light dawned, "so you knew anyhow. You want to try deducing clues on people you didn't have breakfast with."

"Well, anyway," said Jennings, "you know what I mean. How would it be if we practised being detectives? At least," he amended, "bags I be the detective and you can be my assistant."

"But there's nothing to detect," objected Darbishire, "and my father says – "

"Don't be such a saturated wet blanket," Jennings interrupted. "There may be all sorts of things that need detecting – only the eye of the untrained observer can't see them, even though they're staring him straight in it."

"Straight in what?"

"Straight in the eye. Besides, even if there are no murders and things, it'd be spivish useful to find things out about people. We could study chaps' footprints and fingerprints, to begin with.

"And see if they've got any egg stains on their ties. Yes, massive idea," agreed Darbishire, as the tea-bell rang. His eyes shone with enthusiasm as he followed the famous detective into the dining-hall.

2

LN. CT. DET. AG.

Jennings and Darbishire spent most of their spare time the next day in planning the details of their detective organisation, and collecting crime-solving equipment. During morning break they went to the tuck-box room, for Jennings had decided that the best place for their headquarters would be behind the boot-lockers at the far end of the rows of tuck-boxes.

"We must have a headquarters," he explained, "where we can meet and work out clues and things. We might even put up a notice so that chaps will know where to come when they want mysteries solved. Something like *Linbury Court Detective Agency – Chief investigator, J C T Jennings*... And then in quite small letters underneath that," he added as an afterthought, "we might put *Assistant Chief Investigator, C E J Darbishire*."

"Well not too small letters," objected the Assistant Chief Investigator.

They argued for some minutes about the best way to word their notice. Darbishire was in favour of *Families waited upon daily – Distance no object*, but Jennings maintained that *Results guaranteed – Money back if not satisfied* was a more promising way of drawing attention to their services.

"But we aren't going to charge them money," objected Darbishire, "so it wouldn't really be true to say that they got it back, and my father says that truth in small matters – "

"Of course it would be true!" Jennings broke in indignantly. "If we don't charge people we shan't owe them anything if they're not satisfied, and that's what my suggestion means."

They left the text of the advertisement to be settled later on, and set about the more important task of assembling equipment which would be useful in the work of detection. This was easy as they had so little to assemble. From his tuck-box Jennings produced a small telescope, a Morse buzzer and a drooping moustache of ginger-coloured crêpe hair; Darbishire's contribution was a mouth-organ and a pair of toy handcuffs. It was not an imposing collection of scientific aids.

"If only we had a magnifying glass," said Jennings. "Still, I suppose we can make do with the telescope, but it's going to be spivish awkward studying fingerprints through it – we shall have to stand about a hundred miles off."

His assistant picked up the instrument, put it to his eye and peered round in all directions. "It's bust," he announced. "I can only see a sort of inky blackness."

"You haven't taken the metal cap thing off the end, you goof."

"Oh, sorry," said Darbishire humbly.

The Morse buzzer actually buzzed, and would be useful in sending messages for any distance up to about five yards – or rather less as the battery became used up. The moustache was no use – not even as a disguise, for the eye of even the least-trained observer could spot traces of congealed marmalade and the work of moths. And with deep regret they dropped it into one of Venables' football boots, as there was no waste-paper basket at hand. The handcuffs were broken, and both agreed that the mouth-organ served no useful purpose.

"Mind you, Sherlock Holmes was pretty decent at music," said Jennings, picking pieces of fluff from the instrument with his penknife, "so I suppose it might help if I had a bash on this." But Jennings' rendering of "Good King Wenceslas" seemed a poor substitute for Holmes' sensitive fingers coaxing inspiration from his priceless violin.

"For goodness' sake turn it up!" urged the assistant chief investigator as *Deep and crisp and even* went into a jarring discord for the third time. "Fat lot of crimes you'll solve making that row!"

Jennings broke off his musical search for inspiration and slipped the mouth-organ back in his pocket.

"I tell you what," he said. "I vote we practise sending messages to each other in Morse. It's bound to come in useful, and later on, perhaps, we'll invent codes so we can talk to each other without the criminal knowing we suspect him."

Neither of them knew the Morse code by heart, but the alphabet, with the appropriate dots and dashes, was plainly marked underneath the wooden base of the Morse buzzer, and Darbishire found a similar chart printed in his diary. Jennings sat down on a tuck-box with the buzzer in front of him, and his assistant retired to a distance where the sound was just audible. There he stood, alert and ready to check each dot and dash with his chart.

"Get ready," said Jennings. "Message starting now."

A confused buzzing whirred across the intervening space as the chief investigator pressed the control knob of his transmitter. Progress was slow because he had to stop and turn the instrument upside down between each letter, so that he could consult the chart on the bottom. At the receiving end, Darbishire had difficulty in keeping track of anything at all, and complained that Jennings' dots were longer than his dashes. After five minutes' hard work, the buzzing stopped.

"End of message," Jennings announced. "Have you got it?"

"Was the last one but three, a dot or a dash?"

"It was neither really," Jennings confessed. "Actually, it was a space, but I accidentally kept my hand on the tapper while I turned it over. What do you make of the message anyway?"

"It's a bit difficult to say," admitted Darbishire, "but I make it *bip fog nip nop*, and then there's a bit I couldn't quite get, and it ends up *merx pritzh ump thopshozz*. Sounds like Swedish to me!"

"Oh, you're bats," said Jennings irritably. "How could it possibly be that?"

"I thought it might be in code."

"Yes, so it is."

"Well, how can you expect me to work it out if I don't know the code word?"

"Not that sort of code – Morse code," Jennings explained. "It was meant to be – *My name is Jennings. It's a lovely day today* – and the dot at the end was the full stop."

"Oh! Well, either we need more practice, or your Morse code chart is a different edition from mine."

The bell for the end of break put an end to further practice, and it was not until later in the day that the two detectives were able to carry on their preparations. Jennings disappeared after tea, so Darbishire retired to the library, and with his diary in front of him, practised transcribing a magazine article into Morse. It was tiresome work and he was growing weary of it, when the door opened and Jennings appeared.

"I knew I'd find you here, Darbi!" he announced triumphantly, as though he had trailed his friend's footsteps with magnifying glass and bloodhounds. "Look, what do you think about that!"

With a flick of his wrist he turned back the lapel of his jacket, and revealed a small cardboard disc marked *LN. CT.*

DET. AG. in smudged capitals. "And I've made one for you, too," he went on, thrusting a similar disc before Darbishire's peering gaze. "Super decent, aren't they?"

"Coo, yes, spivish!" Darbishire agreed. "I think they're smashing – er – what are they?"

"They're our special secret badges."

"Oh, I see. And I suppose *LN. CT. DET. AG.* spells something in our special secret code."

"No," said Jennings impatiently. "It stands for Linbury Court Detective Agency, and we both pin our badges underneath the lapel of our jackets, so that no one can see them."

"But what's the good of them, if no one can see them?"

"Well, whenever we meet each other, we turn back our lapels and that proves you're a member of the organisation, and you can tell that I'm one too."

"But we know that already," objected Darbishire, " 'cos there's only us two in it, anyway."

His objections were brushed aside and the badge was pinned into place. Then they practised the wrist-flicking drill, until both could prove their membership in a polished, professional manner.

"I thought of another wheeze during afternoon school," said Jennings. "We ought to have a camera, so's we can take photos of footprints and clues and things."

Darbishire nodded and sucked his thumb which he had pricked on the pin of his secret badge. "As a matter of fact," he said thickly, "there's some advertisements for rather decent cameras in this mag I've got here." He removed his thumb and flicked through the magazine, smearing each page with microscopic bloodstains.

"There you are, how about that one!" he said, pointing to the photograph of an expensive-looking model which, the manufacturers informed the world, was the *Grossman Ciné Camera de Luxe. Motion pictures in colour, 16 mm.*

"What's mm.?" Jennings wanted to know.

"It's a thing like centigrades and kilowatts. It means the depth or the height or something," Darbishire explained. "Of course, it's a movie camera really, but that'd be all the better, because supposing we find a suspicious character and he tried to get away, we could follow him and make a film of it; and then perhaps the Head would show it with those educational flicks we have on Wednesdays. Gosh, wouldn't it be super!"

His eyes sparkled excitedly behind his spectacles as he pictured the sensation it would cause. First perhaps, they would have "Plant Life in the Andes" because that was one of his favourites; next say, "Rice Growing in China" because that always turned up in the programme several times a term; and then the epic, epoch-making film of the year, "The Chase and Capture of…" He was hazy about the details, but he had no difficulty in imagining the enthusiastic applause of the audience. He could almost hear their comments in apt, film-trailer language. "It's terrific!" they cried. "It's colossal – it's stupendous – it's the picture of the century!" Darbishire came out of his trance to find that his chief was in full spate.

"…and it would be useful for other things too," he was saying. "We could make an educational slow-motion picture of you doing your maths prep."

"Or a fast-motion one of you eating your tea in gorgeous technicolour," added Darbishire.

"Yes, we mustn't forget the colour!" Jennings' enthusiasm was fired. "We could get Mr Wilkins into a supersonic bate – that always makes him go red in the face, and then we could take a film of him, and the more he got the breeze up, the quicker the colour would change."

They bellowed with laughter at the absurdity of the idea, and then stopped abruptly, as the door hurtled open and Mr Wilkins burst into the library to find out who was making all the noise.

Mr Wilkins was a tall man with a short temper; he made a great deal of noise himself, but he was not particularly pleased when other people did the same.

"What on earth's all this row about?" he demanded loudly. "You know very well that the library is only to be used for silent reading."

"We were just laughing at something we thought of, sir," Jennings explained.

"Well, what was it?" barked Mr Wilkins. "Come along, let's all share the joke, if there is one."

"Actually, sir, we were laughing at – " Jennings began, and then realised that this was an awkward question. Mr Wilkins' countenance was already assuming a delicate shade of pink, and one could not explain that the joke depended upon its becoming pinker. "Well, perhaps it wasn't very funny after all," he amended, "and we didn't really mean to make a noise, sir."

"I can't help what you meant – you *were* making one. This library has got to be treated as a quiet room, and you won't be allowed to use it, if you can't learn to make a noise quietly, like anyone else. Er, I mean, if you can't make less noise."

"Yes, sir."

Mr Wilkins departed, and the quiet of the library was again shattered as he slammed the door behind him with a deafening crash.

Jennings and Darbishire turned once more to the advertisement. It was a beautiful camera and just the thing for detective work, but as Darbishire pointed out, it would probably cost about a hundred pounds, and the two friends could only raise eleven and eightpence between them. There would be no harm, however, in writing for a catalogue as the advertisement suggested. Perhaps the firm made models which were rather less expensive than a hundred pounds – something in the region of eleven and eightpence, say. They took the magazine with them and dashed off to their classroom, where Jennings produced his writing-pad.

"*Dear Sir,*" he wrote, and then stopped, uncertain how to proceed. For some minutes they discussed the correct wording for a business letter of such importance.

"How would it be," Jennings pondered, "if I said – 'Hope you are having decent weather; we aren't.'"

"No," said Darbishire firmly. "Tell him to send a catalogue and ask him how much the cameras are, because we want to buy one."

"But we haven't got enough dosh – we've only got eleven and eightpence."

"Perhaps we'd better leave that bit out then."

"On the other hand, there's nothing to stop me saying I'd *like* to buy one," Jennings argued, "because I would, and anyway that doesn't mean I'm *going* to. And I can't write and say I'm *not* going to buy one, because then he won't send me the catty, and it'd be a super decent thing to have."

Jennings' pen scratched busily for three lines as he made his meaning clear on paper. Darbishire, meanwhile, discovered to his great joy that if he wedged his little finger into the inkpot, he could turn it upside down without the ink spilling. It was a satisfying achievement, until the time came to withdraw his finger. "Oh golly, I'm stuck!" he said.

"Yes, so am I," said Jennings, and laid down his pen.

"I can't just say this – it only takes up about an inch, and Mr Carter says we should never write less than a page."

"But there's nothing else to put," argued Darbishire, forcing his finger out with a plop that sprayed globules of ink over

Jennings' writing-pad, "unless of course, you say what we usually do in our Sunday letter."

"That's an idea," agreed Jennings. "I could tell him we beat Bracebridge School at rugger, and we ought to be practising for the sports next month, only it always rains on half-holidays, so we can't."

"Fat lot he'll care about that!"

"Well, it fills up the page a bit, and then what about hoping he's quite all right. Yours truly, J C T Jennings."

It was not an impressive letter, and certainly not worthy of the proprietor of a first-class detective agency wishing to increase his stock of scientific instruments. And when Jennings had finished blotting Darbishire's ink splashes with his handkerchief, they decided it would not do.

There were half a dozen boys in the classroom, and Jennings decided to enlist the help of someone who possessed greater literary talent. Temple, known as Bod, which was short for Dogsbody, because his initials were CAT, had the best handwriting in the form. He was seated at a desk on the far side of the room, sand-papering the fuselage of a half-built model aeroplane, and he looked up as Jennings charged towards him waving an inky sheet of notepaper.

"I say, Bod, will you do me a favour?" Jennings began, "because you've got a twelve horse-power brain, and you can do supersonic grown-up writing; you know, all slopey and illiterate."

"You mean illegible," corrected Darbishire from the rear.

"Yes, just like grown-ups – that's what I said. You see, I want a catalogue, and I bet the chap won't send it if he thinks I'm just a chap at school, because he'll know I haven't got enough dosh; but if you write it, he'll never guess. Look, here it is in rough, and we want you to make it sound more grown-up!"

Temple's twelve horse-power brain soon grasped what was expected of it, and he stared searchingly at the rough copy that Jennings had written.

"*Dear Sir,*" he read aloud. "*I would like to buy one so how much are they and please send one at once but not if they are more than eleven and eight if so just a catalog. We beat Bracebridge School in the end. There was Sports practics last Wedednesday only there was not any owing to the wet it was scratched. Hopping you are quit all rit. Yours truly, J C T Jennings.*"

Temple raised both eyebrows. "You're bats!" he said. "What on earth does it mean?"

Jennings showed him the advertisement for the *Grossman Ciné Camera de luxe.*

"Oh, I see," said Temple, as light dawned. "But what's all this *quit hopping* stunt?"

"Well, it's only decent to hope he's quite all right," Jennings explained, "and if he isn't – if he's got chicken-pox, or something, he'll be wizard pleased to know that somebody cares about him."

Temple agreed to write the letter properly, and produced a sheet of his own very expensive notepaper. It had *Linbury Court, Sussex*, embossed in tasteful letters, and the school crest, with the Latin motto beneath, on the left-hand side of the paper. Jennings was glad that the heading made no mention of the fact that Linbury Court was a school. He knew from past experience that many firms were not anxious to send their catalogues to schoolboys who had no intention of buying their goods.

"Go away Atkinson and Venables, and all of you. It's private!" Jennings announced, as the remainder of the common room gathered round, eager to know what was happening and show a friendly interest. Temple started work, but he had to keep stopping to push back the crowd which surged round the desk.

"What's the address of this place?" the letter-writer asked. "You have to write it above *Dear Sir*."

"Why, the chap knows where he lives, doesn't he?" asked Atkinson.

"It says the address in the advertisement," Darbishire pointed out. "Somewhere in Oxford Street."

"Good old Oxford!" shouted Parslow with enthusiasm.

"Rotten old Oxford – good old Cambridge!" countered Bromwich major.

"No, they're not then," Jennings joined the discussion group at full volume. "Oxford's miles better! *Cambridge on the tow-path, doing up their braces – Oxford on the river, winning all the races.*"

"No, it's not then," shouted Atkinson. "It's the other way about! It's *Oxford on the tow-path, doing up their braces…*"

"They don't wear braces in the boat race," Jennings argued back, "so that proves you're wrong!"

"Well, a moment ago you said they did! You said *Cambridge on the…*"

"Shut up all of you," yelled Temple, at the top of his voice. "I'm trying to write a letter!"

"Yes, shut up, chaps," urged Jennings, whose voice had contributed most noise to the uproar. He clicked his tongue at them reprovingly. "How can you expect Bod to concentrate with all this hoo-hah going on? Besides, everyone knows that Oxford is gallons better. Mr Carter went to Oxford and Mr Wilkins went to Cambridge, so that proves all oiks are Cambridge."

"And all ruins are Oxford," shouted Venables, and the noise swelled again. "I stick up for Cambridge, Arsenal and Lancashire!"

"And I'm Oxford, Charlton Athletic and Middlesex!" yelled Johnson.

"Shut up!" bawled Temple. In the silence that followed, Darbishire, who had not previously spoken, could be heard murmuring – "And I'm Oxford – "

"Shut up, Darbishire!" shouted the whole room in unison.

"Nobody asked you anyway," added Venables. "You only say you're Oxford because Jennings does."

"No, I don't then," Darbishire defended himself. "I've got a reason. My brother stuck up for Oxford till his last term at school, and then he had the ghastliest hunk of bad luck."

"Why, what happened?"

"He won a Scholarship to Cambridge."

"What filthy, rotten luck!" the Oxford supporters consoled him. "I bet he was fed up."

"He seemed quite pleased actually. Spivish disloyal, I call it!"

"You ought to stick up for Cambridge then," said Bromwich major, scenting a new supporter.

"I know; it's made it jolly difficult for me," Darbishire replied, "but I get over it like this – in boat races and things, I like Oxford to be first and Cambridge second."

In due course the letter was finished and Temple read it out:

"*Dear Sir,*

I am thinking of buying one of your cameras… You needn't actually buy one of course," he explained, "but nobody can stop you thinking about it…*and I shall be glad if you will send me a catalogue…*"

It was a beautiful letter and as Jennings dropped it in the post box, he reflected that it was one step, even though a small one, towards obtaining a first-class collection of crime-solving equipment.

3

The Green Baize Bag

Sports Day at Linbury was always held during the Easter term; for the Headmaster considered that strenuous athletics, in the heat of the summer, was bad for the boys' health, and worse for their cricket. Occasionally, on half-holidays, rugger was cancelled and sports practice was held instead; and it was towards the end of one of these practices, a week after the formation of Jennings' detective agency, that something sensational happened.

Jennings and Darbishire were studying, in a professional manner, the footprints made by the jumpers in the long-jump pit, when they saw a thin, elderly man walking slowly up the drive. There was nothing remarkable about his grey trilby hat and neat blue suit, but he was a stranger and therefore promising material on which to practise deduction.

Jennings saw him first and said: "Now's your chance, Darbi! What facts can you deduce from this chap coming up the drive?"

Darbishire thought hard: "Well," he said, after a pause, "he's not wearing an overcoat and he's carrying an umbrella, so I'd say it must be a warm day and it's not raining."

Jennings expression was scornful.

26

"But we know that already," he said contemptuously. "You don't have to have strangers walking up the drive to know what the weather's like."

"Well, you have a bash if you're so clever," Darbishire muttered.

"H'm!" Jennings summoned up his powers of keen observation. "I'd say he's a piano-tuner, and that he's come to tune the piano."

"Well, of course that's what he's come for, if that's what he is," said Darbishire, with scant respect for his friend's keen observation. "You wouldn't send for a piano-tuner to inspect the gas meter, would you? How can you tell, anyway?"

"You know my methods, my dear Darbishire," the keen observer replied coldly.

"No, what are they?"

Jennings felt that Sherlock Holmes had been fortunate in having a friend who always said the right thing at the right time. Darbishire was a poor substitute for Dr Watson, and the detective's tone was crushing as he explained his reasons. He pointed out that the stranger's hat was just like the hat worn by the man who tuned the piano at Jennings' home in Haywards Heath. Also, the visitor was carrying a green baize bag, which, had it not been empty, might well have held a piano-tuner's tools. Scientific deduction, therefore, proved that he must be a piano-tuner who had forgotten to bring his equipment.

"But if he's forgotten his tools," argued Darbishire, "why does he cart the bag about with him?"

"He probably carries his lunch in it," came the reasoned reply.

"But he must have had his lunch by now; it's nearly three o'clock."

"Of course," Jennings explained patiently, "that's why the bag's empty."

It took his friend a few moments to grasp the flaw in this argument. When he had done so he said: "But a moment ago, you said it was empty because he'd forgotten his tools, and if he'd remembered to put his lunch in his tool-bag it would have reminded him of what he'd forgotten."

"Ah, but what I meant was – " Jennings stopped short, not quite sure what he did mean. Darbishire could be exasperating at times; Dr Watson would never have embarrassed Sherlock Holmes with such awkward questions. He would have gasped with admiration and said: "Wonderful, my dear Holmes, I can hardly believe it!" The trouble with Darbishire was that he could hardly believe it either, only he said so with the wrong sort of expression in his voice.

The stranger had passed them by this time, and was heading for the front door.

"Come on," said Jennings, "let's follow him! Perhaps if we can get near enough, we'll hear him telling whoever opens the door who he is, and then we shall know if I'm right."

They hurried after their quarry, taking care not to draw attention to themselves. Twenty yards from the front door, they took cover behind a holly bush and Darbishire announced: "Look, he's ringing the bell! I wonder what he's come for?"

"Famous detective *you'll* make!" snorted Jennings. "Sherlock Holmes would go and *tell* him what he'd come for, just in case he'd forgotten, along with the tools."

The front door was opened by the housekeeper, Mrs Caffey, known for obvious reasons as Mother Snackbar. After a murmur of explanation, the visitor was admitted and the door closed behind him.

Jennings and Darbishire turned and made for the changing-room. The whistle had sounded, and boys were streaming off the field and dashing towards knee-baths and showers. They were followed, at a more dignified pace, by Mr Hind and Mr Topliss, who had been on duty on the playing field.

Darbishire pondered over the stranger's identity so deeply, as he stood underneath the shower bath, that he turned the cold tap full on by mistake. His shrieks were quickly silenced by Mr Wilkins, who refused to see any difference between shouts of mirth and shouts of agony. Darbishire recovered his breath, stretched for the hot tap and splashed happily.

"You know, Jennings," he said, as his friend appeared, trailing wet footmarks along the duckboards, "I bet you're wrong about that chap. My father says that appearances are deceptive, and for all we know, he's probably someone hefty decent who's come to ask for a half-holiday."

"It's a pity we couldn't see his boots," Jennings replied, looking around vaguely for his towel. "We could have told then. Sherlock Holmes always knew where a chap had come from, just by sitting with half-closed eyelids and seeing what sort of mud he'd got on them."

"But he wouldn't have any," Darbishire objected, "not unless he'd been playing rugger."

"Of course he would! You don't go about without boots."

"No, I mean he wouldn't have any mud on his eyelids."

"I didn't say that, you ancient relic," Jennings answered curtly. To add to his annoyance, he remembered that he had left his towel in the dormitory, and with one eye on Mr Wilkins he started to dry himself on his sweater. A few minutes later, struggling damply into his shirt, he said: "Well, anyway, Darbi, I bet I'm right, and he is the piano-tuner. I bet you a million pounds Mother Snackbar's taken him along to the music room."

Jennings was wrong. Mrs Caffey had shown the stranger into the library, where he handed her a visiting card marked: *H*

Higgins, Jeweller and Silversmith. "The Headmaster's expecting me," Mr Higgins explained.

Mrs Caffey went off to find the Headmaster, and Mr Higgins lowered himself carefully into the depths of a large armchair, and looked around him. The library was a comfortable room, with books shelved all along the oak-panelled walls; not calf-bound volumes with their solemn air of gloomy dignity, but hundreds of carefully chosen books whose authors ranged from Stevenson to Buchan and from Bunyan to Ransome.

Above the oak panelling, hung dozens of brightly coloured shields, bearing the crests of public schools to which the boys of Linbury had won scholarships, and on the mantelpiece over the large brick fireplace stood a row of silver cups. Cricket, soccer, rugger, swimming, boxing, gymnastics – each cup had a ribbon of magenta or white tied round its base, to show which of the two houses had won the trophy at the last contest. In the middle, and overtopping its neighbours by six inches, stood a large, two-handled chalice on which was engraved *Linbury Court Inter-House Sports Cup. Presented by Lieut General Sir Melville Merridew, Ban, DSO, MC.*

Mr Higgins knew the cups well. Every year he engraved "Raleigh" or "Drake" on each, when the winning house had smilingly accepted its trophy from the hand of some distinguished Speech Day visitor.

The door opened and M W B Pemberton-Oakes, Esq, MA (Oxon.), Headmaster, walked in.

"Ah, good afternoon, Mr Higgins."

The jeweller rose to his feet. "Good afternoon, sir," he replied. "I've called for the sports cup."

"Ah, yes," said the Headmaster, taking it down from the mantelpiece. "The cup was won by Raleigh House last year. I meant to ask you to engrave it before, but it slipped my memory. However, there's three weeks yet before our Annual Sports."

"Half an hour will be enough for me, sir," replied Mr Higgins, scribbling "Raleigh" in his notebook. "I'll do it straight away, as soon as I get back to the shop."

"Excellent! And if there's anyone going to the village this afternoon, I'll ask them to call for it."

"Very good, Mr Pemberton-Oakes." The engraver placed the challenge cup reverently in his green baize bag. "Handsome piece of silver, isn't it, sir?"

"Very. It was presented by General Sir Melville Merridew, you know – one of our most distinguished old boys."

"Really, fancy that now!" said Mr Higgins, hushing his voice to a respectful whisper. The Headmaster had made the same remark to him every year for the past ten years, but the jeweller could not have shown more surprise and delight if he had been told that the cup had been presented by William the Conqueror.

Mr Higgins walked back down the drive. He carried the sports cup carefully in his green baize bag, and was quite unaware that his progress was being watched from the changing-room window.

"Look, there's the piano-tuner going back!" said Jennings. He had dressed, and was passing the time, while waiting for Darbishire, by stretching a garter over his head, so that it sat on his scalp like a tight, elastic crown.

"We didn't deduce much from him, did we?" replied Darbishire, searching vainly on the floor for the missing garter.

"No, I suppose not, but... Gosh!" Jennings stopped suddenly and raised his eyebrows in astonishment. The action caused the garter to shoot off his head with a faint *phut*. It described a circle in the air and came to rest at Darbishire's feet. The surprised owner put it on and said: "What's the matter?"

"Gosh!" repeated Jennings. "I say, Darbi, I've just detected a brand new supersonic clue."

"What?"

"That empty bag the piano-tuner's carrying is full!"

"Oh, don't be crazy!" Darbishire hastened to the window. "An empty bag can't be… Oh, yes, I see what you mean."

"I wonder what he's got in it?" said Jennings, his suspicions aroused.

"Perhaps it's his lunch, because you said…" But Jennings was not listening. His keen mind was at work reconstructing the stranger's movements. Mother Snackbar could not have taken him to the music room, for not more than fifteen minutes had elapsed – certainly not enough time to tune two pianos. Well, supposing she had shown him into the library, and had then gone off to tell the Head that a stranger had called. He would have had plenty of time to put one of the challenge cups in his bag, and then walk out of the building before the housekeeper returned. And there was something about the shape of the green baize bag – some hint in the outline made by whatever object was shrouded within; the contours, for instance, of a large silver cup with two handles.

Jennings hesitated no longer. Observation and deduction had pointed the way; the time for action had arrived.

"Quick, Darbishire!" he shouted, his eyes sparkling with excitement. "We must dash up to the library. There's not a second to lose."

Darbishire knew nothing of his friend's train of thought and looked up, surprised. "But I don't want to go to the library," he objected. "I haven't finished reading the book I got out last Sunday. There's 268 pages, and I've only got to page 97, and anyway, it's no good going now because – "

"I'm not talking about changing your book, you twittering nitwit!" Jennings' tone was a mixture of excitement and exasperation. "That chap's a thief, don't you see? He's beetling off with one of our cups in his bag. At least, I think he is, but we'll breeze upstairs and make sure. Come on!"

Together they ran out of the changing-room and up the stairs. As they rounded a blind corner, Jennings collided heavily with Venables, who was walking carefully down the stairs, balancing a board and a box of chessmen on his head. Castles, knights and bishops flew in all directions, but Jennings' errand was too pressing to allow him to stop.

"Sorry, Venables," he called back over his shoulder. "Can't stop now. I'm on an urgent, top priority, hush-hush job."

Venables glowered after the disappearing figures. "You just wait till I catch you!" he cried, and the expression on his face suggested that there would be no hush-hush when it came to telling Jennings what he thought of him.

Up the stairs and along the corridors; Jennings raced ahead and Darbishire panted after him. Soon they reached the library. Jennings flung open the door and rushed in, followed by Darbishire, chattering with nervous excitement.

"It's a good job we didn't waste any time," he was saying, "because my father says that procrastination is the thief of… Jumping jellyfish!" He stopped dead in his tracks and stared at the empty space on the mantelpiece.

"Gosh!" said Jennings. "I was right. He was a burglar!"

His friend gazed at him in round-eyed wonder. "It was super smart of you to spot that bag, Jennings," he said in respectful tones.

"Elementary, my dear Darbishire. You know my methods."

Jennings did his best to look calm and unruffled, but his voice trembled slightly with excitement. "We mustn't stand here nattering," he said. "Let's go after him quick."

"Hadn't we better tell Mr Carter, or someone?"

"We haven't got time. We shall lose him if we don't follow while the scent's still warm."

"Scent!" Darbishire had a fleeting vision of Jennings and himself sniffing their way across open country, like blood-hounds with their snouts to the trail. He giggled, and his friend at once detected his line of thought.

"Oh, don't be so bats, Darbishire," he said. "You know what I mean. We mustn't let the chap get out of sight."

"All right," Darbishire agreed, "but it may be dangerous, don't forget. How do we know this chap isn't a member of an international gang of crooked piano-tuners?"

It was an exciting thought, and Jennings could easily picture the inoffensive Mr Higgins skulking evilly in an ill-lit thieves' kitchen, surrounded by characters from the pages of *Oliver Twist*. As a precaution, they decided to tell someone of their intentions, and as the next person they saw was Venables, they told him.

He marched into the library, smouldering with fury. He had recovered his chess set, and was hot-foot on Jennings' trail. But all thoughts of revenge were forgotten when he heard what had happened.

"And you say the thief's hoofing off down the drive with it," he gasped. "What cheek! Raleigh had to run like mad to win that cup."

"Yes, and if we don't run like mad, they'll lose it." Jennings' tone was urgent as he explained. "It's all right, Venables, all you've got to do is to tell Mr Carter that Darbishire and I are going to do some detective work, and track the thief to his kitchen."

"How d'you know he's going to the kitchen?" Venables wanted to know.

"He must be. If you'd read any good books lately, you'd know that burglars always live in thieves' kitchens."

"Don't the thieves mind, then?"

"Oh, don't be such a crumbling ruin!" Jennings snorted. "They're the same people."

Venables was left with a vague impression of evil-doers swarming round a communal gas oven, as Jennings and Darbishire rushed headlong out of the room.

There was no afternoon school on Wednesdays, and the boys were free to follow their own pursuits until the tea-bell sounded at six o'clock. The detectives had more than two clear hours ahead of them, which should be enough time to bring even the most wily criminal to justice.

Darbishire was worried about leaving the premises without permission but, as Jennings pointed out, they would lose their quarry if they did not start at once, and their disregard for the rules would be forgiven when they returned in triumph. Jennings could picture the scene – the whole school lined up on the quadrangle and cheering wildly as a police car swept up the drive. The two members of the Linbury Court Detective Agency were seated in the back holding the sports cup. As they stepped out of the car they would be greeted by the Headmaster's smile of gratitude. Oddly out of place in the background of the picture, a snarling Mr Higgins was beating his manacled hands vainly against prison bars.

Jennings forced his mind back to the job on hand.

"We shall have to get a move on," he said, as they scampered across the quadrangle. "He'll be nearly at the end of the drive by now."

Darbishire was not a good runner. "Phew," he gasped, "not so fast! I've just thought of something."

"What?"

"Suppose he's got a car waiting for him at the end of the drive. What do we do then?"

Jennings had a ready answer. "We stop the very next car that comes along and say to the driver: 'Quick, follow that car!' That's what 'Dick Barton' does anyway, and it always works."

Darbishire carried his objections a stage further.

"Well, supposing he catches a bus?"

"Then we stop the next one, and tell the conductor to follow the one in front."

This did not satisfy Darbishire. He pointed out that the bus service was limited to one bus every hour, and that as they all went to the same place anyway, there was little point in barking terse instructions at the conductor.

They had rounded a bend half-way down the long drive, when Jennings suddenly gripped his friend's arm, and the next moment pulled him into the thick yew hedge.

"Ssh!" he whispered. "Don't make a noise! I can see him!"

Darbishire glanced nervously over his shoulder. "Where?" he breathed voicelessly.

"He's just turned the corner at the end of the drive."

Darbishire came out of the hedge and removed traces of yew from his collar. "Well, what do we have to whisper for?" he demanded. "The chap's at least two hundred yards away and if he's gone round the corner, he can't see us, anyway."

"We've got to be careful." Jennings' tone was official. Detective-inspector was written all over his features. "It's taking care of little things like that that proves you're a decent detective. Now, we mustn't let him hear us or see us, so I vote we walk on tiptoe and be ready to jump into the hedge if he looks round."

In this fashion they reached the end of the drive, and after Jennings, on hands and knees, had peered furtively round the gatepost, they followed the innocent Mr Higgins along the road to the village.

The only other person in sight was an old farm labourer, flat-footedly trundling a wheelbarrow of leaf mould up the hill, and Darbishire pointed out the significance of this. "Jolly wizard job he hadn't got a fast car waiting for him," he whispered, "because the only next thing that's coming along is that old codger with a barrow, and we'd look silly trying to chase him in that."

They kept close to the hedge, walking in single file. Once Mr Higgins turned to admire the view and the two followers dived, as one man, into the ditch. Although still very muddy, the ditch was not the rushing torrent it had been a week earlier, and when Mr Higgins continued his journey, two bespattered figures climbed out and again took up the trail.

For a hundred yards they tiptoed in silence, their eyes and thoughts fixed on the slim figure in the neat blue suit. Then Darbishire said: "What a rotter the chap must be – pretending to be a piano-tuner and being a burglar all the time!"

"Oh, I soon saw through him," Jennings answered. "Mind you, that story about coming to tune the piano was good enough to take old Mother Snackbar in, but it didn't work with me." He had convinced himself by this time that Mr Higgins' visit had followed, in every detail, the lines which his imagination suggested.

"You know, I had a feeling he was up to no good the moment I saw him," Darbishire remarked confidentially. "In fact, I think I told you so."

"You told me – " Jennings stopped so abruptly that his friend bumped into him. "You told me you thought he was a super decent cove who'd come to ask for a half-holiday."

"Oh," Darbishire smiled wanly. "Anyway, I was right when I told you what my father said about not judging by appearances."

The profound sayings of the Reverend Percival Darbishire were relayed by his son at every opportunity; Jennings, in common with the rest of the school, was beginning to tire of them.

"And I don't think your father's such a frantic brain as you make out," he retorted, "because when we were dashing into the libe you told me your father said that procrastination was the thief of jumping jellyfish. I thought it sounded a bit queer at the time, but I wasn't going to argue, because it was the thief of silver sports cups that I was after."

"I didn't say that," Darbishire protested. "What I said was, my father says that – "

"Well, never mind now," Jennings interrupted. "Come on, we mustn't lose sight of the burglar."

It was half a mile to the village of Linbury, but after they had trailed stealthily for a further hundred yards, Darbishire made a suggestion.

"I say," he said, "must we go on walking on tiptoe? It's super tiring, and I'm beginning to feel like a ballerina."

"All right!" Jennings came down on his heels with a sigh of relief. "I suppose he can't hear us at this distance."

Mr Higgins, being rather deaf, would not have heard them if they had danced behind him in hobnailed boots. He strolled on towards the village, enjoying the peace of the afternoon and blissfully unaware that bloodhounds in human shape were dogging his innocent footsteps.

4

Darbishire Keeps Watch

The village of Linbury, according to the guidebook, lies four and a half miles east of the market town of Dunhambury. Its main architectural features are an early Norman church and a late Victorian horse-trough: the population is three hundred and ninety-eight.

The guidebook says nothing of Linbury as a shopping centre, which is not surprising, for most of the three hundred and ninety-eight inhabitants catch the hourly bus to Dunhambury to make their purchases. There are, however, three shops: *Chas. Lumley – Home-made Cakes and Bicycles Repaired*; *Linbury Stores and Post Office*, which offers a varied stock of goods ranging from caraway seeds to corn plasters; and *H Higgins, Jeweller and Silversmith*. It may seem unusual that a shop with such an imposing description as Jeweller and Silversmith should be found in Linbury, but one glance at the shop window should dispel any idea that it is out of place in such rural surroundings.

When Mr Higgins retired from his jeweller's business in Dunhambury more than ten years previously, he was not happy in idle retirement; so he turned the front room of his house into a small shop, and busied himself in repairing clocks and engraving dog collars. He sold screw-top pencils and butterfly brooches, and as he did not depend upon this for his living, it did not worry him that his customers were few. It was enough, he felt, to justify the sign over his front door. *Jeweller and Silversmith* gave him a comfortable, satisfied feeling whenever he looked at it.

Mr Higgins entered his shop, laid his engraving tools on the counter and set to work on the Merridew Sports Cup. Outside in the village street, Jennings and Darbishire came to a stop, uncertain what to do.

"Golly, isn't this exciting!" Jennings breathed. "I bet Sherlock Holmes wishes he was here. Let's walk past that shop he went into and see if we can see anything. But don't stare at it – just pretend you're out for a stroll."

"Right-o!" Darbishire agreed.

"We ought to go past one at a time, as though we didn't know each other," Jennings continued. "Most detectives do that, so as not to give themselves away, in case anyone's watching. You walk past first and try to look natural, and wait for me by that horse-trough in the middle of the road."

Darbishire was not good at looking natural to order. Normally, people would not have looked twice at this very ordinary ten-year-old boy in a grey suit, with curly hair and large spectacles: but Darbishire tried so hard to appear unconcerned that passers-by turned and stared. Some thought that he had eaten something which had upset him – others, that he must have got his braces uncomfortably twisted across his shoulder blades.

He started off down the street with huge, slow strides, as though he were measuring out a cricket pitch. He felt this to be wrong and changed to quick mincing steps, like a cat on spiked railings: he was conscious of his arms swinging like pendulums from his shoulders, and he had a feeling that his hands were swelling to the size of boxing-gloves. He put his hands in his pockets, wondering why it was that they felt so clumsy; then his left ear started to itch – a thing that never happened as a rule. "Gosh, what a bish I'm making of it!" he thought. "I can't scratch it yet – it'd look funny." But his itching ear allowed him no peace, and he jerked his hands clear, scattering the contents of his trouser-pockets all over the road.

After that, he tried marching with head erect, but people were beginning to cast suspicious glances, and he found himself lunging forward, left arm with left leg – right arm with right leg. What on earth was the matter with him? He never made bishes like this during PT! He changed step two or three times, but it was no use. After a very artificial journey he reached the horse-trough, and suddenly remembered that he had been too flustered to notice the jeweller's shop at all.

Jennings joined him a few moments later. "What on earth's the matter, Darbi?" he demanded. "You went prancing down the street like a crab with chilblains. You couldn't have drawn more attention to yourself if you'd hopped like a kangaroo!"

"Sorry, Jen."

"Now," said Jennings, getting back to business. "I've discovered something that might be important."

"Yes?" Darbishire was eager again, now that his ordeal was over.

"The shop's called H Higgins, Jeweller and Silversmith."

"That's a spivish feeble sort of clue," observed Darbishire, who had been expecting a revelation.

"Oh, is it? That just shows how much you know! Why does he call himself Jeweller and Silversmith, then? You answer me that, if you're so clever. Why not just – piano-tuner?"

"Because he isn't a piano-tuner," returned Darbishire logically.

"Exactly. I knew he wasn't all the time, and this proves it."

"No, you didn't. You said he was one at first."

Jennings clicked his tongue with impatience. "I know I did, but that was because he was *pretending* to be a piano-tuner, don't you see? But if he really *was* one, he wouldn't paint it up over his shop, in case Mother Snackbar saw it when she went to the village."

Jennings' clear reasoning was too deep for Darbishire, who by this time was floundering out of his depth.

"So you think he really is a piano-tuner who's pretending he isn't?" he asked.

"Yes," said Jennings decisively.

"But a moment ago you said he wasn't. You said he was just pretending to be one."

"Oh, you're bats," said Jennings, and wisely decided to let the point drop. "Anyway, we know now that he's a jeweller."

"Real or pretending?"

"Pretending of course. Yes, that must be it! He pretends to be a jeweller so that he can trade in stolen watches and things."

They sat on the edge of the horse-trough while they thought this out; then Jennings said: "Gosh, yes, it all fits in! I read a story once, where the police raided a jeweller's shop, but they heard them coming and hid all the booty in a trice."

"Hid it in a what?"

"A trice," Jennings repeated. "I suppose it's a secret cupboard, or something – the book didn't say."

"And you think this Higgins chap has got a trice hidden away in his shop?"

"Bound to have."

They sat silent for a few seconds and then Jennings rose to his feet. "What I ought to do now," he announced, "is to try and find some evidence."

"Yes, good wheeze," Darbishire agreed. "How are you going to do it, though?"

"I haven't a clue."

This time it was Darbishire's turn to speak his mind. "Well, of course you haven't," he said, with surprising heat. "If you had, you wouldn't have to find any."

"I didn't mean that," returned Jennings, "and don't get in a flap – I'll think of something."

Jennings wondered what Sherlock Holmes would do. Probably he would keep watch, and note any suspicious comings or goings. He might even disguise himself as a road sweeper or a pedlar, so that he could loiter without, arousing any comment. A pedlar would be better, because then he could go inside the shop pretending to sell his wares. The scheme had obvious drawbacks, but as he could think of nothing else he suggested it to his assistant.

Darbishire thought it was an excellent idea. He knew that after his recent performance, he was not likely to be cast for a role that demanded much acting talent, and that the difficult part would have to be played by Jennings.

"Okay, then," he said with enthusiasm. "I vote we do that. Let's be pedlars – or rather, you be a pedlar."

"That's all very well," Jennings replied, "but what could we peddle?"

"Bicycles?" suggested Darbishire brightly.

"Oh, don't be such a crumbling ruin," snorted Jennings. "You don't peddle bicycles!" And after a pause he added: "Well, you do, of course, but not that sort of peddle. Anyway, I should look daft as a pedlar – they're usually ragged blokes in dirty clothes."

Darbishire looked at his superior shrewdly. "That's just how you look," he said encouragingly. "What a good job that ditch we took cover in wasn't quite dry. And you tore your pocket on the hedge so – "

"No," said Jennings firmly. "Let's think of something else."

At length he produced a foolproof idea. He would walk boldly into the shop in the guise of a customer, and see if his trained eye could pick up any clues. Darbishire was to keep watch outside, in case the bogus jeweller became suspicious and tried to escape. As an excuse for loitering, he could pretend to be an artist busily painting the village street, with the ornamental horse-trough in the foreground. Jennings produced a blue crayon and the back of a letter, as the artist's stock-in-trade.

Darbishire was appalled.

"But I can't draw horse-troughs," he protested. "I can only draw aeroplanes."

"Well, draw aeroplanes then."

"But there aren't any, and anyway, you know how people come and look over artists' shoulders while they are working," he went on, bolstering up his objection. "They'd know I was a fraud then."

Jennings brushed this flimsy argument aside. "If they do that," he said, "you can say you've just done a lightning sketch of an aeroplane that's just flown over, and that now you're going to draw a horse-trough underneath."

"Yes, but – "

"Oh, don't be so feeble, Darbishire! You've got miles the easiest job; and anyway, if the worst comes to the worst, turn the wretched aeroplane upside down and pretend it's a horse-trough. They'll just think you're one of these super modern artists."

"Oh, all right." Darbishire resigned himself to his fate. "I suppose I might as well have a bash at it." After all, his was the easier task. He felt faint with nervousness when he thought of the risks that Jennings would have to undergo. "What are you going to do when you get in the shop?" he asked, in a voice which he was unable to keep steady.

Jennings had it all worked out. He would go in and look round the shop, jingling the fourpence in his trouser-pockets to give the impression that he was a customer of some substance. He would examine any priceless jewels which happened to be lying around, and then he would casually lead the conversation to the subject of silver cups. "I shall try and frighten him," he decided.

He damped his handkerchief in the horse-trough and sponged the mud from his knees. A wealthy customer mustn't look as if he had recently emerged from a ditch. "I shall say," he went on in official tones, "that a silver cup has been stolen and that certain clues have led me to form a tent – er, a tent – something."

"A tenterhook?" suggested Darbishire, feeling that this state of suspense summed up the situation neatly.

"No, a – a tentative theory, that's it."

"But that won't help," his assistant objected. "He won't give it back to you."

"I know, but I shall be watching him carefully. Perhaps through half-closed lids even, and if he goes pale and starts suddenly – "

"Starts what suddenly?"

"Not starts anything." The detective's voice grew edgy with exasperation. "I mean if he stops short in his tracks, and then starts guiltily."

Darbishire wondered how anyone could stop in their tracks before they had started, but he didn't like to say so, for Jennings' expression was forbidding. He explained that, if the outcome of the stopping and starting test was satisfactory, he would hasten out of the shop and try to find a policeman. If, meanwhile, the criminal tried to bolt, Darbishire must take up the chase and bring him crashing to the ground with a low rugger tackle.

Darbishire gulped hard and swallowed. He said he was not much good at rugger.

"Well, a moment ago you said you were feeble at art," Jennings replied. "You'll wizard well have to pull your socks up if you're going to help. We can't afford to make a bish of our first case."

He strode off towards the shop; his heart was thumping heavily and he had an uncomfortable feeling in the pit of his stomach, but he was not going to let his assistant know that he felt nervous.

Darbishire watched him go, and then turned his attention to art. It was half-past four and beginning to grow dark – not the best time of day for an artist to start work out of doors; but on the other hand, the failing light would conceal the worst defects of his drawing. He held his crayon at arm's length and shut one eye, measuring the proportions of the horse-trough. Then he drew three jet-propelled fighters, with machine-guns blazing and aviators descending by parachute. Ack-ack fire was bursting all over the picture, with dotted lines indicating the paths of the exploding shells. It bore little resemblance to the village street of Linbury, even when turned upside down, but it was the best he could do. Fortunately, no one seemed to be taking much notice.

He worked on, colouring the aeroplane wings with thick blue shading, and wondering what was happening to his friend. Gosh! it was hairy daring, walking bang into a thieves' kitchen like that! Jennings must have supersonic, ice-cold nerves! What if the burglar attacked him? What if, at this very moment, he was in a perilous plight? Supposing... Darbishire's train of thought suddenly veered off the rails, as he looked up to discover that he, also, was in a perilous plight – or soon would be.

A herd of cows was lowing its way up the village street. A thirsty herd, too, for as soon as the animals sighted the horse-trough, they made for it, as one cow. Unlike most artists who prefer to sit well away from their model, Darbishire was perched on the edge of the object which he was supposed to be drawing. He could not retreat without losing sight of H Higgins' shop door, and he was hemmed in on the other three sides by the trough and the cows plodding thirstily towards it.

Darbishire was fond of most animals, but cattle did not appeal to him. Now, it seemed, he had suddenly become the hub of a large herd, all pushing and jostling and looking forward to a long, satisfying drink.

"It's all right," he told himself. "Cows don't hurt you – unless they're bulls."

Cautiously he tried to edge his way to safety, but his escape was cut off by two lively heifers who drank their fill from the trough, and spilt what they did not want over Darbishire's feet. At every moment he expected them to tread on his toes or lean on him, for these cows were not the bashful kind, who shy at the approach of a human being. Waving tails flickered before his eyes and put a stop to any pretence of going on with his drawing. "Oh, gosh, this is awful!" he thought. "How can anyone expect art to flourish in the middle of a frantic hoo-hah like this?"

A small boy in a torn jersey came up. He was brandishing a stick and was obviously in charge of the herd. He shouted, "Giddup, giddup, will you!" and obediently the cows started to move on. "It's all right, mate, they won't hurt you!"

Darbishire tried to look as though no such thought had entered his head; but he was secretly envious of one so young, whose orders were so promptly obeyed.

The last cow finished her drink and stared over Darbishire's shoulder at the picture which he was still clutching in his hand.

She did not appear to think very highly of it as a work of art, for she lowed at it in a melancholy fashion, and wandered off to join the rest of the herd.

"Phew!" murmured Darbishire. "Why do these things always pick on me to happen to?" Then his thoughts returned once more to his colleague. "Golly! I'd clean forgotten about old Jen! I hope nothing dreadful's happened."

Nothing dreadful had. As Darbishire stared anxiously in the direction of the shop door, it opened, and Jennings appeared. He was carrying the Merridew Inter-House Sports Cup under his arm.

"Jumping jellyfish!" shouted Darbishire, in amazed delight. He was so surprised that he nearly toppled backwards into the horse-trough.

5

Triumph and Dismay

Jennings had been feeling distinctly nervous when he had first entered Mr Higgins' shop. An electric bell rang shrilly, and kept on ringing while he stood on the threshold, holding the door ajar. With some misgiving he shut it, and approached the counter.

"Have you any, er – ?"

The shop was stocked so modestly that it would sound out of place to ask to be shown priceless jewels. His trained eye roamed round in search of some other object, and fell upon a pair of cheap ear-rings fastened to a card.

"Have you any ear-rings?" he mumbled, feeling rather silly.

Mr Higgins, being slightly deaf, thought that he was being asked for key-rings. "Yes," he said, groping beneath the counter. "I've got some very nice ones here. Just the thing for a lad like you."

"Oh, they're not for me," said Jennings hastily, and felt his courage ebbing. "I want them for, er – well, it doesn't matter really. I think I'll leave it, if you don't mind."

H Higgins, Esq, Jeweller and Silversmith, gave him an odd look and, for a moment, he panicked.

"What I mean is, I want them as a present for someone else," he went on wildly, hardly conscious of what he was saying. "Someone who isn't here, and I don't know what sized ears they take – I mean I don't even know whether they've got any already, so it doesn't matter, thanks all the same."

Mr Higgins stared at Jennings over the top of his spectacles. "Speak up, laddie," he said. "I'm a bit hard of hearing – who is it who hasn't got any ears?"

Jennings clutched the counter and tried to control his emotions. "This won't do," he told himself, "you're making a most frantic bish of things! For goodness' sake pull yourself together! Sherlock Holmes wouldn't let himself get rattled like this." He took a deep breath, and began again.

"Well, I – er, the point is," he said, "I'm making some inquiries about a silver sports cup belonging to Linbury Court School."

He watched Mr Higgins narrowly, but the jeweller did not blench; neither did he start violently nor stop dead in his tracks. Instead, a slow smile of understanding lit up his features.

"Linbury Court, why of course! Yes, I've just done it."

Jennings was surprised. "You – you admit it then?"

"It's quite ready," returned Mr Higgins brightly. "You've come to take it away, I suppose?"

"Well, yes, but I – I hardly expected you'd give it up as easily as all that."

Mr Higgins produced the newly-engraved cup and wrapped a layer of tissue paper round it. "Mind you," he said roguishly, "I wouldn't give this cup to anyone who just walked into the shop and asked for it. Might be a thief, see!" He shot his head forward to make his point clear and Jennings recoiled, fearing some trick. "But I know a bit about thieves, see, being a jeweller," he said, with a crafty wink.

"Yes," Jennings gulped, "I'm sure you do!"

The situation was getting out of hand. Mr Higgins was not behaving at all in the way that any self-respecting criminal ought to behave. A horrible doubt came into Jennings' mind. Perhaps Mr Higgins was not a thief after all! Perhaps there was some explanation for this extraordinary game that the jeweller was playing with school property! Jennings could not think what it could be, for it never entered his head that the man had any connection with the names "Drake" and "Raleigh" engraved on the cups. With an effort, he forced his attention back to what Mr Higgins was saying.

"Oh, yes," the jeweller replied. "I know quite a bit about burglars and their little ways – and about detectives too. Take Sherlock Holmes for example!" He pointed to a shelf, high up on the wall behind the counter. Sandwiched between table napkin rings and cut-glass cruets he had found a place for his favourite books, and Jennings could see *A Study in Scarlet*, *The Memoirs of Sherlock Holmes*, and *His Last Bow* amongst a dozen or more detective novels.

"Now, Sherlock Holmes has taught me a few things; and as soon as you mentioned Linbury Court, I knew at once that you weren't an impostor. And how did I tell that?" he asked, with a cunning smile.

Jennings made a last, half-hearted attempt to frighten Mr Higgins into a confession of guilt. "I suppose your conscience must have told you?"

Mr Higgins laughed merrily.

"My conscience! Good gracious, no! Whatever makes you say that?" He dropped his voice to a low conspiratorial whisper. "I'll tell you. It was your school tie and your school socks. That proved you were genuine. That's deduction, see?"

Jennings took the cup from Mr Higgins and walked out in a daze, trying to piece together the ruins of his shattered theories.

It was almost dark when they made their way back from the village. Jennings was strangely silent, searching for some reasonable explanation of Mr Higgins' conduct. But Darbishire was bubbling over with excitement, and demanding details.

"But what happened?" he persisted, for the sixth time. "How did you manage to get it back? Did the chap put up much of a struggle?"

"Well, actually," Jennings replied slowly, "I think I've made rather a bish of the whole issue. You see, I'm not even sure that he is a burglar, now."

"You mean he used to be one, and now he's given it up?"

"No, I don't think now, that he ever was one."

"But he must be," Darbishire proclaimed with emphasis. He was not going to allow any feeble anti-climax to spoil the events of the afternoon. "Dash it all, Jen, he pinched the cup, didn't he?"

"Yes, I know," said Jennings, still very puzzled, "but he gave it back without any hoo-hah. He even seemed to expect that someone might come and ask for it."

This time it was Darbishire's powers of deduction that provided the explanation. As they trotted along, he pointed out that the whole business was a gigantic bluff. As soon as Mr Higgins was aware that Jennings knew his guilty secret, he realised that the game was up. What else could he do, but hand the cup back, and pretend that the whole thing had been an unfortunate misunderstanding?

"You frightened him, you see," he explained. "He knew wizard well that if he hadn't given it back, you would have had the police on him like lightning. For all he knew, the building was surrounded already – perhaps he even saw me keeping watch and thought I was – " He left the sentence unfinished. Even in his state of flushed excitement, he knew that no one could have mistaken him for a plain-clothes policeman.

There was certainly something to be said for Darbishire's argument, and as it seemed to be the only solution, Jennings was forced to admit that he had been deceived by the jeweller's clever acting.

"Yes, of course," he said. "I never thought of that! Gosh, Darbishire, I've been swindled!"

Darbishire pressed home his advantage. "He must have taken you for a chump," he said with relish. "I bet he's laughing his head off now. I bet they all are!"

He drew a lively picture of the thieves' kitchen behind Mr Higgins' shop. Crafty, low-browed desperadoes were slapping their knees and rolling about, helpless with mirth.

Apart from this, however, they both agreed that the expedition had been a success. The stolen cup had been recovered, and the detectives could return to school well satisfied with their work.

It was quite dark when they reached Linbury Court. They had hurried so that they should not be late for tea at six o'clock, and they arrived with half an hour to spare. The first person they met was Binns minor, the youngest boy in the school.

"Gosh," he squeaked in his shrill, Form I treble. "You two are going to cop it! Old Wilkie's on duty, and he's been searching the building for you. He guessed you'd hoofed out without permish, and he's in the most supersonic bate. I bet he sends you to the Head, and then – pheeew – doyng! Pheeew – doyng!"

His sound-picture of a visit to the Headmaster was most life-like, and he skipped happily along the corridor, *pheeew-ing* and *doyng-ing*, and swishing the air with a bootlace.

Jennings was not worried. "It's all right, Darbishire. Wait till they know what we've done for them," he said, and together they made for the common room.

Here, their welcome was more satisfying; Venables, Temple, Atkinson, Bromwich major and a dozen more crowded round

53

in enthusiastic greeting. Venables had told them of the burglary and the pursuit. He had sworn them to secrecy, so that small fry such as Binns minor, and similar persons of low estate, should not have the pleasure of knowing that something sensational was afoot.

"What happened, Jennings?" they all shouted at once. "Did you catch him?" and then, as they caught sight of the cup bursting through its layer of tissue paper, a long gasp of amazement ran round the room.

"Gosh, it's the sports cup!" breathed Venables.

"Golly, super daring!" Atkinson's eyes shone with admiration.

"What happened? However did you get it back?" Temple wanted to know.

Jennings could not resist the temptation to bask in well-earned glory. "Elementary, my dear Temple," he said, a smile playing round the corners of his mouth. "You know my methods. I tracked the burglar to his den. It's not too difficult, if you're any good at detective work."

"Yes, it was wizzo," added Darbishire, "and I disguised myself as an artist and drew aeroplanes, so that people wouldn't suspect."

"Wouldn't suspect what?"

"That the horse-trough was really three jet propelled fighters, upside down."

Nobody knew what Darbishire was talking about, and they pressed for details.

"Well," said Jennings, "I just walked into the thieves' kitchen, and spoke to the chap like Sherlock Holmes would have done. And he got the wind up and gave it back without a struggle."

"What's a thieves' kitchen like?" Venables had been trying all afternoon to picture domestic arrangements beyond the reach of the law.

"They vary quite a bit," Jennings informed him, from his superior knowledge. "This one had got ear-rings."

"Gosh, how spivish!" Venables promptly added seafarers and gipsies to the staff of his kitchen. He could almost hear the jangling of the gold circlets hanging from their lobes, as his criminals bent over their pastry-boards and frying-pans.

"Did you tell Mr Carter what had happened?" Jennings asked him.

"No," said Venables. "I couldn't find him. I think he must have gone out. I did try and tell Mr Wilkins, but he got in a bate and wouldn't listen properly. I told him about the crook and all that and he said: 'Cor-wumph! Don't come bothering me with cups and cooks and kitchens. Can't you see I'm busy?' "

There was no doubt that Jennings' first exploit as a detective had been a great success. The group of boys stood round the smiling sleuths and showered congratulations on them. Fantastic prices were mentioned as the reward that the Headmaster would certainly feel called upon to make, when the bogus jeweller was behind prison bars.

The common room rang with shouts of lavish praise.

"Good old Jennings! Good old Darbishire! Three cheers for the Linbury Court Detective Agency!"

Jennings and Darbishire, bursting with pride and trying to look modest, enjoyed their moment of glory. But it was over all too soon, for half a minute later Mr Carter walked into the common room, and tried his hand at deduction.

He had just come back from Dunhambury in his car, and was on his way to his room, when the excited hubbub told him that something unusual had taken place. In two seconds he was surrounded by a throng of boys, each one raising his voice in an effort to drown his colleagues and be first with the news.

"Sir, please sir, something super exciting has happened, sir," shrilled Atkinson.

"Yes, sir – there's been a rather decent burglary, sir," called Bromwich major.

"But it's all right, sir," added Temple, "because we've got it back, thanks to Jennings. He's super at sleuthing sir, isn't he, sir?"

"Be quiet!" said Mr Carter softly, and immediately the room became silent. "I haven't the slightest idea what you're talking about," he went on. "Twenty people jabbering away at once isn't the best way of sorting things out. Come along, Jennings, you tell me what it's all about."

Holding the sports cup lovingly in his arms, Jennings recounted the afternoon's adventures. When he had finished, Mr Carter said: "Well, well, poor Mr Higgins! He little knows the commotion he's caused."

"What do you mean, sir?" asked Venables.

Mr Carter did not reply. Instead, he took the cup from Jennings and looked at the words engraved on the front.

"There you are, you see, sir," Darbishire chimed in, fearful lest he should be denied his share in the glory. "It's the sports cup all right, isn't it? Are you going to tell the police, sir?"

"I hardly think that will be necessary, Darbishire," Mr Carter returned gravely.

"Oh, sir, you must!" pleaded a dozen voices. "Otherwise, sir, all Jennings' famous detective work will be wasted."

Jennings looked hard at Mr Carter, and suddenly detected a look of amusement which the master was trying to suppress. All at once his doubts returned. He knew now that there was something suspicious about the whole affair. It had been too easy.

"I agree with Mr Carter," he said, to the surprise of the crowd. "We've got the cup back – that's the main thing, and besides, the burglar wasn't such a bad old stick. I thought he was quite decent, all things considered."

Mr Carter smiled and said: "I should go even further than that, Jennings. I should say that your burglar was the most obliging thief you could possibly hope to meet."

The crowd continued to gape. They, too, sensed by this time that all was not as it should be, and listened with breathless expectancy as Mr Carter went on: "He's even taken the trouble to engrave last year's winner on the cup he stole." He pointed to Raleigh and the date, which everyone knew had not been on the cup when they had last seen it.

There was a painful silence, and then Jennings said slowly: "Oh... I see... So I did make a bish of being a famous detective after all!"

"I'm afraid so, Jennings."

The boy tried hard to hide his disappointment. "Well," he said, unhappily, "all I can say is, I'm jolly glad Sherlock Holmes won't get to hear about it!"

Then the tea-bell rang. The tension broke and roars of laughter swept from the lips of the crowd as the explanation became clear. But Jennings and Darbishire were not laughing. They followed the hilarious crowd to the dining-hall, wondering what on earth they could say when confronted by an angry Mr Wilkins.

6

Further Outlook – Unsettled

There was, of course, trouble. Mr Wilkins took a serious view of their leaving the school grounds without permission, and reported them to the Headmaster.

"Just like Old Wilkie," sighed Jennings, as they, walked with dragging footsteps towards the study. "I bet Mr Carter wouldn't have kicked up such a supersonic hoo-hah, if he'd been on duty."

Binns minor danced light heartedly behind them: "Pheew... doyng!" he prophesied with a gay smile, and then turned and ran to the shelter of his own form room.

Jennings said: "Don't take any notice of those Form I ruins. We'll deal with Binns later." They were both wearing an extra pair of underpants, but this precaution proved unnecessary; Mr Pemberton-Oakes left his cane in his cupboard and talked ...and talked.

"I have noticed for some time," he was saying twenty minutes later, "that your interests are becoming lawless and unrestrained. Instead of going quietly about the building like members of civilised society, you charge like an armoured division, mouthing mechanical engine noises. The energy which you should be devoting to organised games is being wasted in worthless horse-play. It is little more than a week since I had occasion to speak to you about your unseemly conduct at the chessboard. Little did I think that my remarks would pass unheeded; little did I think that…" And on…and on.

Jennings and Darbishire listened dutifully for the first fifteen minutes. After that their faces paid attention, but their minds were unable to cope with the ceaseless flow of words. Jennings counted the flowers on the patterned wallpaper behind the Headmaster's head. There were twenty-five in each row and forty rows in all, so that made… His eye was fixed steadily on the Headmaster, but his brain was busy with mental arithmetic. Darbishire picked out random words from the torrent swirling about his ears; with his finger he traced the outline of each letter on the seam of his trousers, but his gaze never shifted from the tortoiseshell spectacles on the Head-magisterial nose.

After thirty-five minutes they were allowed to go. Binns minor was lurking near the study door with his ears tuned to catch any sound of *pheew-ing* and *doyng-ing* that might come from within. It was not that he bore Jennings and Darbishire any ill-will, but if these unpleasant things were going to happen anyway, he wanted to be the first to know about it.

"Oh, well," said Darbishire, as they prepared for bed later that evening. "I suppose we've had it now. I didn't listen to all he said, but I had a sort of feeling that he might get into a bate if we did any more famous sleuthing."

"He never said that." Jennings put his spare underpants back in the drawer. "He said – well, I can't remember either, but I'm sure he didn't mean we've got to pack up the detective agency."

He was more determined than ever to carry on, because Venables and his friends had wasted no time in spreading the story of Jennings' "frantic bish" all over the school, and wherever he went he was greeted with shouts of derision. It was the joke of the term and Form III enjoyed it to the full.

During the next few days Jennings managed to rouse Darbishire's enthusiasm once again, and together they made up endless codes and copied them down in their diaries. Then they practised sending each other code messages while Mr Wilkins was taking their form, but even this turned out disastrously.

Mr Wilkins took Form III for geography. His methods were vigorous and his voice was loud. He strode about the room dictating notes at shorthand speed and demonstrating the rotation of the earth with a large, faded globe.

Jennings sat in the back row and stared out of the window. He was half a page behind with the dictated notes, so he gave up struggling and decided to copy them out afterwards. Surely, he thought, there must be some way of proving his detective skill! He brooded over this for some minutes and could spare only a small part of his brain for Mr Wilkins' demonstration of how the earth goes round.

"Now, look at this globe carefully," boomed Mr Wilkins, "and you'll see that these lines going round the earth, North and South of the Equator, are lines of latitude – or parallels as they are sometimes called. And these others are longitude lines and they go round from North to South and meet at the Poles. All clear?"

"Yes, sir," chorused the form.

"Good. Now for six months of the year as the earth spins round, the North Pole is pointing away from the sun – like this." Mr Wilkins gave the earth a vigorous tilt and slapped it smartly in the Pacific Ocean, so that it creaked round protestingly on its rusty axis. "So, although it's turning round once in every twenty-four hours, it's always dark in the North Polar regions and light at the South Pole. And vice versa for the other six months."

"You mean it goes round as it's doing now, only it doesn't squeak?" asked Darbishire.

"Exactly. And if the earth were not tilted like this" – Mr Wilkins defied the laws of Nature and made the earth upright – "then we should have twelve hours' day and twelve hours' night all through the year. Is that clear?... Rumbelow?"

"Yes, sir."

"Do you understand, Temple?"

"Oh yes, sir."

"Jennings?"

Jennings was still looking out of the window.

Hawkins, the night watchman, was crossing the quadrangle with a heavy tread. He was known as Old Nightie and the boys saw little of him, for his labours started when they were safely in bed. With his hunched shoulders and drooping head he looked an odd sort of character, and he had a habit of shooting stealthy glances in all directions whenever he spoke. Jennings had met him occasionally, emerging from the boiler-room, but had not paid much attention to him. Of course, it was possible that he was just an innocent old...

"Jennings!" repeated Mr Wilkins in a voice which would have shattered the deepest day-dream.

"Oh, er – I beg your pardon, sir."

"Corwumph! Wake up, boy. I asked you if that was clear."

"Oh, yes, perfectly, sir, thank you," replied Jennings politely.

"Then perhaps," said Mr Wilkins, in persuasive tones, "you'll be good enough to explain it to me."

"But you know it already, sir."

"Of course I know it already," barked Mr Wilkins, and the persuasive tone had vanished. "I wouldn't be asking you if I didn't know, would I?"

"You mean the other way round, sir," suggested Darbishire, helpfully. "You *would* ask him if you *did* want to know, wouldn't you, sir. But you don't really want to know, sir – you just want to know if he knows."

"I… I… Corwumph! Of course I don't really want to know – that's why I'm asking – I mean… Well anyway, what did I say?"

Jennings thought hard. "You said that longitude and latitude are a lot of lines which are parallel and they meet at the North and South Poles, sir."

Mr Wilkins turned three shades pinker. "But, you silly little boy, if they're parallel, how on earth can they meet?"

"I thought, perhaps, that was one of the things you wanted to know, sir." And then, as Mr Wilkins began to *Corwumph* again, Jennings hastened on: "Well sir, I think why these parallel lines meet is because the earth goes round all tilted."

"Corwumph! you haven't been listening to a word I've said."

"Oh, yes, sir, I heard it all, sir," Jennings assured him. "You said that the real reason that causes the earth to go round is the rotation of the earth, sir, and if it didn't it would be night and day both at the same time."

Mr Wilkins clutched his head in his hands and Jennings hurried on, anxious to show how much he had understood: "And it would be versa-visa – er – viva voce, sir, for the rest of the year, because the earth takes six months to turn round every twelve hours, and the other six months it turns round the other way, sir."

"I… I… I…" Mr Wilkins swallowed hard, summoned up his reserves of patience and marched to the blackboard where, with brisk bold strokes of the chalk, he started his explanation all over again.

Jennings listened carefully for a few minutes, but the picture of Old Nightie, with his shambling flat-footed gait and furtive expression, floated back into his mind. Mr Wilkins, now hoarse with explanation, was dashing off sketch maps on the board and Jennings took advantage of this lull to take his diary from his pocket. After consulting the key, he wrote a note in his secret code, rolled it into a small pellet and flicked it with his ruler towards Darbishire in the second row. Unfortunately his aim was poor; the pellet soared far beyond the target area and landed on the master's desk.

"Oh, gosh," he groaned in dismay. "It would have to go and pancake, bang on the top of the control tower."

Mr Wilkins, busy at the blackboard, saw it too, but for the time being he affected not to notice it. When he had finished his sketch map of the earth and the sun, he turned from the board and walked straight towards the master's desk.

Jennings froze, and then breathed again as the master turned away without seeming to see the pellet. Mr Wilkins spent the next two minutes walking up and down past his desk, and Jennings' heart missed a beat every time the footsteps turned about. Would he see it, or wouldn't he? The suspense was unbearable. But Mr Wilkins' volcanic manner concealed a kind heart; he hated to see boys suffer, so he put Jennings out of his misery by discovering the note the next time that he passed. He unfolded the paper and saw a collection of letters, figures and signs of the zodiac scrawled all over it.

"Who wrote this?" he demanded.

Jennings' hand went up. "Please, sir, I did."

"Oh, did you? And will you come up here and translate it, so that all may enjoy the benefit of your artistic efforts."

Jennings came with a heavy heart. He knew Darbishire wouldn't laugh, but he didn't want to give the rest of the form a chance to repeat their jeers at his expense. For a moment he was tempted to pretend that his message referred to the previous Saturday's rugger match, but he was a truthful boy so he took a deep breath and translated: "Do you think Old

Nightie is an escaped convict? I do," he read aloud, feeling rather foolish.

Form III was delighted.

"Oh, sir, make Jennings give his reasons, sir," they pleaded.

"Well, go on, Jennings," barked Mr Wilkins, determined to get to the bottom of it. "Why do you think Old – er – why do you think Hawkins is an escaped convict?"

"Oh, I don't, really, sir," Jennings said uncomfortably. "It was just an idea. You see, good detectives always make inquiries about suspicious-looking characters, sir, and Nightie's got a funny way of looking at you, so I thought he'd be a good chap to practise detective work on, sir. He…well, that's all, really sir," he finished lamely.

"But… Corwumph, you silly little boy, Hawkins has been night watchman here for nearly forty years."

"Yes, of course, sir, I'd forgotten that."

"Now, look here, Jennings," said Mr Wilkins, "we've had quite enough of this detective nonsense. It's interfering with your work and causing a lot of trouble all round. Any more of this and you'll find yourself in serious trouble. Do you understand?"

"Yes, sir," said Jennings sadly.

He was given an hour's detention for flicking the pellet, but it was not this that distressed him – it was the continued sniggers of his colleagues, who seized on the instance as a further excuse to laugh at his efforts.

"It's no good, Darbishire," he said, as they sat in their headquarters in the tuck-box room after school. "There's just nothing here that needs detecting. We might as well be living in a concentration camp for all the fun we get."

Someone had scrawled *Ha, ha, ha!* right across the notice advertising the *Linbury Court Detective Agency*, and Jennings snatched it down and threw it into the wastepaper basket.

Their detective equipment, which they had collected with such pride, seemed to mock them. The glass had fallen out of the telescope, the battery of the Morse buzzer had run down and the mouth-organ would make no sound, since it had been accidentally dropped in the wash-basin. There was, of course, the illustrated catalogue of the *Grossman Ciné Camera Co, Ltd*, which had arrived a few days after they had written for it. Jennings glanced through its pages. It was a beautiful catalogue, and they had spent hours poring over the illustrations of the cameras advertised between its glossy covers.

"Gosh, that's a super one," said Jennings, pausing once more to admire a ciné de luxe model priced at ninety-five guineas. "If only we'd got that!"

"But we haven't," Darbishire pointed out, "and if we had, I don't see that it'd be any good, if we've got no crimes to use it on."

"Well, it'd come in handy for other things," Jennings argued. "Sports Day, for instance. I could take a photo finish of you winning the half-mile."

He roared with laughter at his joke, and Darbishire gave him a bespectacled blink of reproach. "You needn't make a joke about it," he said.

Darbishire's entry for the half-mile open was considered to be the second funniest joke of the term. He was no athlete; when he joined his fellows in a practice run, he would finish the lap panting and exhausted, a hundred yards behind the leaders. He clenched his fists and threw his legs high into the air behind him, but for all his efforts he moved at the pace of a penguin prancing amongst the Antarctic snows.

"It's jolly well not fair to laugh," he complained, as Jennings tossed the catalogue back into the tuck-box. "I can't help it if

I'm a bit slow. Some chaps are good at one thing and some are good at others, and my father says – "

"And what are you good at?"

"I'm good at – well, I'm good at other things, and anyway, I don't like running. I'm only going in for the half-mile to help win the sports cup for Drake."

"Coming in last won't help much."

"There's always a chance," Darbishire defended himself. "Supposing, say, Bod gets measles the day before, and MacTaggart sprains his ankle in the high-jump, and then perhaps, for instance, if it was a hot day and Nuttall got a touch of sun-stroke, because he does sometimes – "

"You're bats!" Jennings interrupted. "The only way you could win would be if Mr Carter accidentally shot everyone else in the foot with the starting pistol. Dash it all, Darbi, you couldn't beat a performing seal running on its flippers."

Darbishire sighed. If only he could run like Jennings, who was an easy favourite for the 440 yards and the long-jump, under twelve.

"My father says – " he began, and then trailed off as he had forgotten which wise saying of his father's had occurred to him. Instead, he began replacing their useless equipment in the tuck-box. "Come on," he said, "let's put all this junk away and go for a practice run round the field. If Drake doesn't win the cup this year, no one can say it's because I didn't practice hard enough."

7

Jennings Sees the Light

It was a week later when Jennings first saw the light in the sanatorium. He awoke unexpectedly to hear the school clock striking eleven, and slipped out of bed to fetch a drink of water.

Tooth-glass in hand, he stood looking out of the dormitory window in the direction of the sanatorium on the far side of the quadrangle. It was a two-storeyed, detached building and a light was shining from a ground-floor window. As he watched, a shadow passed across the blind; head and shoulders were clearly outlined, as the figure stood, for a moment, before the window.

"Someone must be ill," he decided. "Glad I'm not Matron – beetling about taking temperatures at this time of night." He finished his drink, tumbled back into bed and was soon asleep.

The next morning during class he suddenly had a thought. This was unusual in itself, for Mr Hind's arithmetic period seldom provoked him to mental effort; but his idea had nothing to do with the problem which they were studying, of how long it would take to fill a tank with water flowing in through pipe A and pipe B, while at the same time it was pouring to waste through pipe C. Instead, it was an idea full of exciting possibilities. No one was ill; there had been no absentees at the morning roll call. Why then, should Matron, or anyone else, be casting their shadows on the blind of the sanatorium late at night?

He urged his reasoning powers a step further. Surely, the figure at the window could not have been Matron, for she always wore a flowing nurse's head-dress, and the shadow on the blind had been a clear-cut, bareheaded silhouette. The more he thought of it, the more convinced he became that the unknown profile was that of a man. It had not looked like the Head, or Mr Carter, or any of the masters; perhaps it was a burglar, perhaps...

Mr Hind's soft, purring voice caught his ear.

"Have you finished that sum yet, Jennings?" he cooed.

Jennings glanced at the page before him. "No, sir," he confessed. "I haven't actually quite *finished* it yet, sir."

"How much have you done?"

"I haven't actually quite started it yet, sir."

"Too bad, too bad," murmured Mr Hind, but no one was deceived by his soothing manner; it was known that Mr Hind could pounce like a hawk out of the clear blue sky, when he felt so inclined.

"And why," he inquired, "have we not actually quite *finished* it yet?"

Jennings thought rapidly. "Well, sir, it doesn't really make sense. You see, if you wanted to fill this tank and you turned on pipe *A* and pipe *B*, you'd put the plug in if you had any sense, so it wouldn't keep running out of pipe *C*, sir. I mean, you'd be crazy if you didn't, wouldn't you, sir?"

Mr Hind remarked that he was not aware that there was anything wrong with his mental powers.

"Oh, I don't mean *you* would be crazy, sir – I mean anyone would. And even if they hadn't got a proper plug they could bung up pipe *C* with a handkerchief or a sponge, or something, and that'd make the sum come out ever so much easier, sir."

"Jennings," said Mr Hind sadly, "you are an illiterate nit-wit, an uncouth youth, a sub-human relic; in short, my dear boy, you are a miserable specimen." And with that he passed on to Darbishire, who informed him that the answer came to approximately seven years, one week, four days and twenty-three seconds.

Mr Hind did not blink. "The right answer," he purred, "is twelve and a half minutes."

"Oh!" Darbishire seemed surprised. "That puts me a bit outside the target area, sir. It's just as well I said my answer was only approximate. May I have a mark for scoring a near miss, sir?"

The lesson dragged on. Jennings tried hard to cope with the antics of imaginary plumbers turning taps on and off for no apparent reason, but the shadowy figure at the sanatorium window kept appearing in his mind's eye.

He made a beeline for Darbishire the moment the lesson was over.

"Listen," he said, urgently, "I really think I'm on to something supersonic at last." The confident note was back in his voice again, and his eyes sparkled. "I woke up last night and had a dekko out of the window, and what do you think I saw?"

"Old Wilkie dancing in the moonlight," answered Darbishire facetiously.

"Oh, don't be so feeble! This is the real thing – at least, it might be. I'll tell you what I saw" – he paused dramatically. "I saw a light in the san."

"Well, what of it? I expect Matron forgot to turn it off."

"We'll soon see about that," said Jennings. "Come on, we'll go and ask her."

Mystified, Darbishire followed the confident footsteps of his chief up to the door of Matron's sitting-room on the first floor.

"You wait here," Jennings whispered. "I'm going to make some inquiries."

He returned a few minutes later wearing a wide, satisfied smile, and said: "Matron didn't go into the san at all last night, because I asked her. What's more, we haven't had a mump or a measle all the term, so no one's been over there except one of Mother Snackbar's sewing-maids. She counts the laundry, or something, but she's only there in the daytime – I found that out too."

"Yes, but what's all this leading up to?"

"Well, I shouldn't be surprised if the chap I saw was a – " He stopped. He'd been going to say "burglar" but his recent experience had taught him to be careful of using such a description lightly. "My theory is," he went on, "that tramps have been using the place to sleep in. They could easily find out that no one ever goes there at night, unless they've got the measles, so why shouldn't they do that."

"Why shouldn't the tramps catch the measles?"

"No, you bazooka. Why shouldn't they sleep there?"

"I can think of several reasons," objected Darbishire. "First, they'd be more comfortable under a hedge than they would be on hard school beds, and secondly – "

"Well, it needn't be tramps," urged Jennings. "It could be army deserters or – or escaped convicts even."

Darbishire giggled. "Like Old Nightie?"

"Oh, don't be bats! Anyway, if Old Nightie was any good at his job, he'd have seen the light himself. I bet he was snoring his head off down in the boiler-room."

"Did you tell Matron about your theory?" Darbishire asked.

"Of course not. This is a man's job. There's no point in frightening the women about it." He drew himself to his full height – a chivalrous guardian of the weaker sex. "I just sort of led the conversation round to it, and I found out that the masters never go over there either; they can't without her knowing, because they haven't got a key!"

This last argument swayed Darbishire. "Golly," he said, "sounds as though we're on to something, doesn't it?"

"Pity we can't get in and investigate," Jennings mused. "Never mind, let's go and have a look at the outside, and see if we can spot anything suspicious."

"Hadn't we better tell Mr Carter? Remember what a frantic bish we made last time."

"All in good time," replied the chief of the detective agency. "It's no good telling Mr Carter until we've got proof."

They ran down to their headquarters to collect their equipment, and then crossed the quadrangle and stood staring at the creeper-covered walls of the sanatorium. It had originally been a large cottage, but as it stood well away from the main building, it made a suitable place to isolate boys when they were ill. Two upstairs rooms were used as wards for the patients, and a bed-sitting-room on the ground floor provided for the needs of a night nurse. In case of emergency, she could telephone to the main building by means of a private wire.

Only one room was in daily use, except in times of epidemic; this was on the ground floor next to the night nurse's quarters, and here Ivy, the sewing-maid, darned socks, sewed on buttons and sorted the laundry.

She was rather surprised, on looking out of the window, to see that her movements were being watched from the quad. Jennings, a battered telescope to his eye, was surveying the cottage walls searchingly. His work was hampered by the fact that the lens kept dropping out, but he persevered, screwing up his nose and baring his teeth in an effort to improve his vision.

"Well, I like their cheek," bristled Ivy and pulled down the blind. She could not afford to waste time on Tuesday mornings, for she worked to a strict routine. On Tuesdays she checked the soiled linen: and packed it into the large laundry baskets; on, Wednesdays she had only to add the boys' pyjamas to the top of the pile, and the baskets were ready for the laundry van's weekly visit.

When she pulled up the workroom blind, a few minutes later, she noticed that the two keen observers had gone. They were holding a council of war in the privacy of their headquarters; for although nothing had been learned from their close scrutiny of the cottage windows, Jennings was already planning the next move.

"I've got a cracking idea!" he said. "We'll keep watch, and if we see the light again we'll hoof over to the san and spy on the tramps red-handed. Then we can beetle down to that telephone box at the end of the drive and dial 999."

"Coo, yes, spivish decent wheeze," agreed Darbishire.

"And we'll take cricket stumps, or hockey sticks, or something in case we're attacked, and we'll let ourselves out of the dormitory window on the fire-escape lifeline."

"Wouldn't it be easier just to walk down the stairs?"

"I suppose it would, really. I never thought of that," Jennings confessed. The staircase as a means of descent seemed rather dull compared with the fire-escape, but he didn't press the point. "Anyway," he said, "we can both see the san windows from our beds, so we'll keep watch by turns. You stay awake tonight until it strikes ten, and then wake me up."

This plan was found to contain one serious flaw when they tried it out. With the best will in the world, Darbishire was unable to keep his eyes open until ten o'clock. It was warm between the blankets, and he felt sleep creeping over him when he had been on duty for half an hour.

"Gosh, this won't do," he told himself. "There's always the most frantic hoo-hah if sentries go to sleep at their posts." He strained his eyes towards the unlighted cottage. "Now whatever I do, I mustn't go to sleep," he murmured, and the next thing he knew, the rising bell was shrilling its morning message, and shafts of sunlight were playing on the dormitory wall above his head.

Jennings was furious.

"You great, crumbling ruin," he complained. "You've gone and bished things up again! If you were in the army, you could be shot at dawn for doing a thing like that."

"Sorry, Jen," said Darbishire humbly.

"Not this dawn, of course," Jennings corrected, "because that's been over for about a hundred years. It's too bad, Darbishire. There we were, fast asleep, and for all we know the san was knee-deep in trespassers tramping all over the place."

"You mean tramps trespassing, not trespassers tramping."

"Don't quibble. You've made a frightful bish and you're about as much use as a radio-active suet pudding."

"Sorry, Jen," Darbishire said again, as he got out of bed and reached for his slippers.

"Now, tonight," Jennings decided as they stood at the wash-basins, "there'll be no nonsense. We'll do it the other way round, and I'll take first watch."

When Jennings had been on watch for forty minutes he began to realise that his criticism of Darbishire had been rather harsh. It was more difficult to keep awake than he had thought. "It's because I'm too comfortable," he told himself. "If I got out of bed, I'd be too cold to fall asleep."

For five minutes he stood at the window and shivered; his bare feet on the linoleum grew so cold that they ached, so he put on his slippers and dressing-gown. Three minutes later he added his top blanket, and shortly after that he decided that standing up was adding unnecessarily to his suffering. "After all," he persuaded himself, "horses go to sleep standing up, so I might, too, if I don't look out."

He compromised by kneeling on the foot of his bed with his elbows resting on the bed-rail, his chin cupped in his hands. And it was in this strange, doubled-up attitude that Mr Carter found him, fast asleep, when he walked round the dormitories at ten o'clock.

A further meeting of the detective organisation was held the next afternoon.

"It's no good this trying to keep awake," the chief detective explained. "We'll have to think of something else."

The meeting was silent while the members thought. Then Jennings had an idea, and the wide-awake look came back into his eyes.

"I say, Darbi," he said, "I think I've got it. If we had an alarm clock, I could set it for eleven o'clock, and fix it on to my ear by tying my braces round my head." He waved his hands vaguely round his ears by way of explanation. "Then I could sleep on one side and put my pillow on top of it."

"Why do all that?"

"So's to soften the noise when it goes off. We don't want Venables and Co. getting out of bed, thinking it's a fire practice." He lowered his voice: "Besides, Mr Carter might hear. He's got supersonic earsight."

"I see. Yes, quite a massive wheeze." Darbishire gazed at his friend admiringly. "But suppose you fell out of bed, or turned over in your sleep – you might bust the glass."

"No, I shan't," his chief explained, "because when I've tied it on, I shall lie on my side, and you can tie my hands to the bed-rail with my tie, so that I can't turn over." For some minutes they debated the point of how he was to switch the alarm off with his hands securely tied, and eventually it was decided that Jennings, wakened by the alarm, should call quietly to Darbishire in the next bed. His assistant would then leap nimbly from sleep, and report for switching-off duty.

"All right then," agreed Darbishire, rising from his tuck-box. "Let's do that – it'll be a cracking priority prang. Do it tonight, shall we?"

He made for the door with the air of one whose problem had been neatly solved. He could always trust his friend, when it came to thinking out a really first-class, foolproof plan.

Jennings called him back. "There's just one snag," he said slowly.

"Surely not," said Darbishire. "What is it?"

"We haven't got an alarm clock!"

The question of how they were to wake was shelved for the time being, as there seemed to be no obvious solution. Perhaps it would just happen, Jennings thought optimistically, and they passed on to the next stage of their preparations.

"What we ought to do," the senior detective decided, "is to write a note, in case things go wrong, and we have to be rescued."

"Oh, golly, is it going to be as dangerous as all that?" Darbishire enjoyed making plans; it made him feel important, and as there was a good chance that they would never be carried out, he could plot with ruthless daring. But suddenly he wondered what would happen if this scheme ever became a reality. He was secretly appalled at the idea of invading a sinister sanatorium, bristling with hostile trespassers.

"I think we ought to tell Mr Carter at once," he demurred, "because my father says it's better to be safe than sorry, and I think he's right."

Jennings was scornful. The time to tell Mr Carter would be when they had proved beyond doubt that their suspicions were justified.

"It'll be all right," he added confidently. "We shan't come to any harm if we leave a note, because that tells them where we've gone, and then they can surround the place with flying squads and things. I read a book once, all about a chap who was going to another chap's house, but he didn't trust this chap, the first chap didn't; so this first chap gave a note to his butler, and if he hadn't come back to his house by next morning, he was to take it to Scotland Yard."

"Who was to take what?"

"The butler was to take the note that the chap gave him. And when…"

"Yes, but what's the point of telling me all this?" Darbishire interrupted. "Even if we wrote a note like this chap did, we haven't got a butler to give it to."

"But you don't *have* to have a butler," Jennings explained patiently.

"You said we did."

"No, I didn't. I said that's what the chap did. The first chap, I mean, not the chap whose house – "

"All right, all right, you needn't go through it all again," protested Darbishire. "I don't think much of this scheme anyway – we haven't got the right sort of gear. First, we haven't got an alarm clock, and now we haven't got a butler. I'd like to see how your first chap would have got on if he'd only had a busted telescope and a dumb mouth-organ to help him."

"Okay then, we won't bother about the note," Jennings agreed. "We'll just tell someone we're going – someone we can trust, of course, because the whole thing's got to be kept super-spivish secret."

They decided that Venables could be trusted not to reveal their plan. Jennings had not really forgiven him for his gibes of the previous week, but, as he explained to Darbishire, someone had got to be in the know, in case the worst happened.

That evening, after tea, Venables sat in his classroom, making spectacles with twisted pipe-cleaners. He made one pair and put them on, and was busily engaged on the second when he heard his name being breathed in a hoarse whisper. He peered through the glassless rims which sat drunkenly on his nose, and saw that Jennings was beckoning to him to come into the corridor. Several times during the day, Jennings had been on the point of taking Venables into his confidence, but always someone had approached within earshot and the attempt had been abandoned. Jennings was taking no chances, and Venables was unable to discover the reason for the furtive stage-whispers, until they reached the tuck-box room. Then Jennings spoke:

"I say, Venables, will you do me a super cracking favour? Do say yes!"

Venables had been caught that way before. "If you mean will I swap you my ten-cent Liberian three-cornered stamp – "

"No, no, it's not that."

"And I'm not going to lend you my spiked running shoes either."

"Not that sort of favour," said Jennings. "It's the san. I've seen lights there and I think it's tramps, and Darbishire and I are planning to go over and investigate one night, only we don't know when, yet. If we don't come back, we want you to go and tell Mr Carter."

"Gosh, how super!" breathed Venables. His eyes lit up behind his wobbling pipe-cleaners. One eyepiece was twice the size of the other, and the white fluffy rims gave him something of the appearance of a giant panda.

He absorbed such details as Jennings was able to give, and returned to his classroom, flushed with the joy of knowing an important secret.

8

Mr Wilkins Grows Curious

Venables did not really mean to give Jennings' secret away; but as the evening wore on, he found it more and more difficult to keep the news to himself.

"If only Atki knew what I know," he thought, as the dormitory bell rang, "I bet he'd be surprised!" For although Venables had only a minor part to play, he knew that he would come in for a certain amount of reflected glory if he told Atkinson. And after all, Atkinson was his best friend – he wouldn't let it go any further.

As he washed his knees, Venables had a short battle with his conscience; then he approached his friend and said in a hushed undertone: "I say, Atki, what d'you think?"

"Oh, buzz off, Venables," retorted Atkinson. "You're always coming round asking me what I think. How do I know what I think if you don't tell me? If you think I can guess what I'm supposed to be thinking when I haven't even got a clue – "

"All right then, I won't tell you, but you'll be sorry. I shouldn't be surprised if you lived to regret it, even, especially as it's an urgent hush-hush job like invasion plans and things."

"What is?"

"I shan't tell you. You told me to buzz off."

"Okay, I take that back," Atkinson compromised. "Tell me – go on, be decent."

" 'Fraid I can't; it's lethal confidential."

"But a moment ago you said – " Atkinson began, and then changed his tactics. "Look, if you tell me, I'll put you on my cake list."

"But you haven't got any cake!"

"Maybe not. But that's no reason why I shouldn't make a list of chaps I'd like to give a hunk of cake to if I *had* got any."

"Well, promise you won't split?" And after Atkinson had solemnly agreed, Venables dropped his voice to the right pitch for revealing secrets. "Well, what do you think?" he began.

Atkinson threw a wet sponge at him. "That's what you said before," he stormed.

"Oh, sorry," said Venables and started off again. It was a good secret as it stood, but Venables could not resist the temptation of adding a few details of his own.

"Jennings and Darbishire think they're tramps," he finished up, "but I shouldn't be surprised if they're spies who've landed on the beach, and are hiding in the san because it's nice and quiet; but you won't tell anyone, will you?"

Atkinson sat next to Temple in the dining-hall. Next day at lunch he said: "I say, Bod, I've heard something – it's massive daring."

"I suppose you've been ear-wagging again," returned Temple shortly. He was bolting his suet pudding as fast as he could, and keeping one eye on Matron who was dealing with second helpings. There were only a few portions left, and he would have to clear his plate like lightning, if he was going to achieve the second helping that he hoped for.

"No, I haven't honestly," protested Atkinson, "but Jennings has seen lights in the san and Venables thinks it's spies, but I've got a better idea."

Atkinson's theory was that black marketeers were using the unoccupied wards as a warehouse; he drew a vivid picture of the rooms crammed with rare valuables. Boxes of four-bladed penknives were stacked on the floor; model yachts and batting-gloves lay piled on the beds; rare stamps and model locomotives were scattered in all corners of the room.

"Mind you, I don't know," he admitted. "It's just what I think. And you won't tell anyone will you, because it's a hefty rare secret?"

Temple had been so interested in the news that he had unconsciously slowed down the pace of his eating. He glanced at Matron and saw, to his horror, that the dish containing second helpings was empty.

"Oh, gosh," he groaned, "and I'd have given anything for a refill of that suet! It was the wizardest muck we've had this week."

His only consolation was that he knew a secret. It would be quite safe with him; he would never dream of telling a soul – except of course Parslow, because Parslow could be trusted not to spread it – beyond, perhaps mentioning it to Martin-Jones, who was a close friend. Johnson received a garbled account from Martin-Jones, and Bromwich major heard the news from Johnson; then it spread via Nuttall, Brown major, Thomson minor, Rumbelow and Paterson, until the information was shared by three-quarters of the school.

Venables sat in his classroom that evening after tea; he was wearing his pipe-cleaner spectacles and making pipe-cleaner poodles. Binns minor, who usually chose to be a jet-propelled aircraft at that time of day, flew in at desk-top level. Spotting Venables through his bomb-sights, he banked sharply, throttled back his engine with a sharp snap of his teeth, and circled down to make a perfect landing on the runway between the desks.

"I say, Venables, have you heard about the light in the san?" he shrilled importantly.

"Of course I have – I was the first one to know. It's hairy stale buns by now. It's supposed to be a corking secret, but if it gets round like this we might as well have it broadcast on the six o'clock news." He was annoyed to think that such a closely guarded secret should be common property. How could it have leaked out?

"I think it's a bit thick, the way chaps can't keep their mouths shut," Venables grumbled on, eyeing the jet-propelled Binns minor with distaste. "I know all about it because Jennings told me himself. He said I was the only chap he could trust, and now even Form I knows."

Binns minor immediately put his finger on the flaw in the security measures.

"Who's told everyone? You have!" he squeaked in triumph.

"I only told Atkinson – he's not everybody," Venables answered reasonably. "Anyway, the damage is done now. The only people who don't know about it are the masters. Thank goodness they've got no way of finding out!"

Mr Carter laid his newspaper down when he heard the heavy footsteps approaching his room. He knew from past experience that reading was out of the question, when Mr Wilkins decided to pay him one of his tumultuous visits.

A sound like a naval twelve-gun salute signified that his visitor was knocking, and the next moment the door shuddered on its hinges, as Mr Wilkins burst into the room.

"I say, Carter, I've discovered something you ought to know about," he began, as though he was addressing a vast, open-air meeting. "Jennings has seen lights in the sanatorium, late at night."

"Yes, I know," Mr Carter murmured gently.

"You know?"

"Everybody knows by now, don't they? And if they didn't know before, they can probably hear you telling me all about it."

"Sorry, old man, was I speaking loudly?" Mr Wilkins had a voice like a loud-hailer, but now he lowered his tone as though adjusting the knob of his volume-control. "I heard Thomson minor and Rumbelow whispering away in the changing-room, at the tops of their voices. Sounded like a particularly confidential secret, from the row they made over it." He thudded heavily into an armchair, and the protesting springs twanged like a harp. "Who told you anyway?" he demanded, as the music died away.

"Nobody told me," replied Mr Carter, hoping that his armchair would stand the strain. "I deduced it. I happened to be in dormitory four when someone mentioned the word 'sanatorium.' There was a sudden, deathly hush, and everyone looked at me and then looked away again quickly." Mr Carter smiled. Because he had let the incident pass without comment, it was mistakenly supposed that he had not noticed anything unusual.

"Well, I'll tell you another thing," said Mr Wilkins earnestly. "Jennings has seen tramps going in and out of the back door – or so Rumbelow says. Time something was done about it, don't you agree?"

"No, I don't think I do," replied Mr Carter unexpectedly, as he filled his pipe. If only Wilkins would go, he could get on with his crossword puzzle.

"You – you mean to sit there and tell me that you don't propose to do anything about it?"

"Quite right."

Mr Wilkins leapt to his feet to the accompaniment of a deep musical note from the springs of the armchair. "But good heavens, Carter," he expostulated, pacing up and down the room, "this is a serious matter – how serious, you don't seem to realise."

He emphasised his point with a sweeping gesture which brought a tobacco jar crashing down on top of a record that lay on the radiogram. "Oh, sorry, old man," he apologised, gathering up the broken pieces and dropping them on the fire. "Never mind, it was only an old record... Now what was I saying? Oh, yes. This is a serious business. If tramps are using the sanatorium to sleep in, it's a matter for the police."

"I don't think we'll bother the police just yet," returned Mr Carter. "There's quite a simple explan – " He broke off, sniffed the air keenly, and glanced towards the fireplace.

The gramophone record was giving off a stream of dense smoke, and fumes of burning wax were filling the room. Mr Carter seized the coal tongs and shovel, grabbed the flaming fragments and threw them out of the window, on to a flowerbed below.

His expression had lost some of its usual calm, when he returned to his chair. "Now, look here, Wilkins," he said. "This sanatorium business is nothing to worry about, and anyway, I'm extremely busy. At least, I intend to be busy doing a crossword puzzle. Do you mind leaving this matter in my hands?"

"Yes, but dash it all, Carter," protested Mr Wilkins. "You can't let tramps use the place as an hotel – think of the damage! They've probably been stealing the furniture. I shouldn't be surprised if the place has been practically emptied already!"

Mr Carter picked up his newspaper and said: "You know, Wilkins, you jump to conclusions just as Jennings does. However, if it will give you any satisfaction, we'll take a stroll over there at eleven o'clock, and you can see for yourself."

"Yes, but – "

"Eleven o'clock," replied Mr Carter firmly, and turned to his crossword puzzle.

A gust of wind like the slip-stream of an aircraft, followed by a thunderous crash, denoted that Mr Wilkins had swept out of the room, and slammed the door behind him.

At eleven o'clock he was back, bursting with suppressed excitement. "They're there," he announced dramatically. "The light's on in one of the downstair rooms!"

Mr Carter sighed. He had not quite finished his crossword puzzle.

Together they descended the stairs and crossed the quadrangle, Mr Wilkins tense with expectation and Mr Carter wearing an amused smile.

The front door was open and they went in. A light was shining from a crack beneath the sewing-room door and Mr Carter put his hand on the doorknob. "Don't be too violent with the tramps, will you, Wilkins?" he said in tones of mock gravity. He opened the door and Mr Wilkins hurried into the room.

"Oh!" he said.

Old Nightie, armed with a mop, was polishing the linoleum with soft, gentle strokes, as though afraid of wearing out the pattern. He looked up, surprised, for he seldom had the pleasure of welcoming visitors.

" 'Evening, Mr Carter, sir, 'evening, Mr Wilkins," he said, and leaned heavily on his mop-handle. "Anything I can do for you, sir?"

"It's all right, thank you, Hawkins," returned Mr Carter. "Mr Wilkins wanted to assure himself that all was well. He thought you were – "

"I – I – well actually, as a matter of fact, Hawkins," Mr Wilkins interposed quickly. "The point is, if you follow me – " He stopped, uncomfortably aware that Old Nightie did not follow him. The old man was giving him one of his queer looks, and Mr Wilkins cast a despairing glance at Mr Carter, who obligingly came to his rescue. He explained to Old Nightie that the sanatorium lights were the subject of strange rumours among the boys. "I thought I'd let you know," he continued, "because there's a remote chance that one or two of them might decide to investigate at first hand. If they do, I want you to let me know at once. You can phone through to my room from the night nurse's quarters next door, and I'll come over and deal with them."

"Yes, sir," replied the night watchman, his thin, wrinkled face creasing in a wide smile. "Well, fancy them thinking that! Why, I've been sweeping up over here regular as clockwork for thirty-nine years, and we haven't had a tramp or burglar in all that time. Ten forty-five on the dot, I finish down the boiler-room, pick up the key and over I come – bar when there's anyone ill in bed, of course."

He straightened his back and looked round the barely-furnished room. "I reckon as a burglar would have to be pretty hard up before he came to the san," he grinned. "There's nothing here worth pinching."

He waved his mop towards a small table, on which were stacked a hot-water bottle, two packets of cotton-wool, an ear-syringe and several rolls of bandage. The laundry baskets, a chair and Ivy's sewing materials were the only other objects in the room. "Don't you worry, sir, we shan't get troubled with no burglars breaking in here."

"Satisfied, Mr Wilkins?" his colleague asked.

But Mr Wilkins was not entirely satisfied. As they crossed the quadrangle on their way back, he demanded that Mr Carter should ban amateur detectives' games altogether. "Put your foot down firmly," he urged. "You're Jennings' housemaster. Tell him that all this nonsense about deducing clues has got to stop; and take those Sherlock Holmes books away from him, too."

"It was I who introduced him to Sherlock Holmes," Mr Carter observed, "so I can't very well forbid it. Besides, so long as he's only *playing* at detectives it can do no harm, and if you stop them playing one sort of game, they'll only think up another one."

He knew from experience how true this was, and he decided that his best course was to keep a finger on the pulse of Jennings' activities, without drawing everyone's attention to them. "Don't worry, Wilkins," he advised, as they entered the main building. "While Jennings is puzzling over the lights in the cottage, he's not likely to turn his attention to anything worse."

"But supposing they go over there? They're always devising wild and impossible schemes, you know."

"They can scheme till they're black in the face," said Mr Carter, "provided they don't actually carry them out; and I don't think they will – they can't keep awake long enough, for one thing."

Mr Wilkins suddenly stopped, turned to his colleague and slapped him heartily on the back. "Carter," he said, "I think it would be a good thing if they *did* carry their plans out. Might curb their taste for adventure. If they go over there and find it's only old Hawkins after all, they'll feel a bit sick, won't they?"

"Just as you did," Mr Carter interposed. He had not quite recovered from the slap on the back.

"Never mind about me," Mr Wilkins put in hastily, "but these silly little boys have made such a fuss over this secret discovery nonsense, that if it turns out to be a damp squib it'll put paid to the whole business. And then, perhaps, Jennings will get his mind back to doing a little more work in class, and the whole school can look forward to a spot of peace."

Mr Carter did not agree with this easy solution. "Oh, no," he said. "We can't actually let him go over there – that would never do. But you needn't worry, Wilkins, it won't come to that."

"It'd be a good thing for the whole school if it did," his colleague answered. And, as it happened, he was right. But Mr Wilkins had no notion of just how accurately he had hit the nail on the head.

9

Jennings Makes an Entrance

The green of the playing field was sprinkled with the white shorts and running vests of seventy-nine boys practising for the sports. There was one week to go before Sports Day on the following Wednesday, and now that half-term had passed and the weather was kinder, the boys were determined to make the most of their opportunities to practise.

Sports Day was not, however, a formal occasion attended by a large crowd of parents, for March is never a good month for outdoor social gatherings. The custom was to regard the event solely as an athletic contest, which parents might attend if they wished, but only those who lived close at hand were expected to do so.

In the long-jump pit, Binns minor was happily building tunnels in the sand, and leaping for his life every time a jumper hurtled past the take-off board; Atkinson and Venables were practising starts on the hundred yards track, and the Raleigh and Drake relay teams were perfecting the difficult task of passing the baton without losing speed.

Jennings finished the last few yards of the "220" at top speed, and then went to look for Darbishire. He found him at the high-jump standards. With gritted teeth and fingernails dug deeply into the palms of his hands, he was vainly trying to jump over the bar, which rested three feet from the ground.

Darbishire felt that he could clear this height easily, if only he could decide which leg to hurl into the air first. Whichever way he tried, he always arrived at the point of take-off with the wrong foot foremost, and had to turn himself round in mid-air like a ballet dancer.

"Gosh," said Jennings, as he watched his friend's efforts to become airborne. "You're hopeless! You look like a pelican trying to take-off on an ice rink."

Darbishire rubbed his bruised knees. "Well, it doesn't really matter," he replied, "because I'm not, going in for the high-jump – I'm just going to concentrate on the half-mile."

This was the longest track event in the programme and Darbishire had entered for it as he felt that any shorter race would be over before he was properly off the mark. There was also the advantage that, as only six boys had entered, it would not be necessary to run heats, and Darbishire knew that he could not be weeded out of the running before the great day dawned. "I'm going in for the egg-and-spoon race too, of course," he added, "because sometimes, the slower you are the better chance you've got, and as I'm miles the slowest I might win. Gosh, I wish I could run like you though, Jennings!"

Jennings sat on the high-jump landing-mat and took his shoes off. Venables had a pair of proper spiked running shoes, and as he was Jennings' closest rival in the 440 yards under twelve, this advantage gave Jennings much food for thought.

"How would it be," he pondered, "if I bunged some drawing-pins through the soles of my gym shoes? Would that turn them into spiked running shoes, d'you think?"

Darbishire agreed that it might be a good idea, provided that he remembered to stick the pins through the right way round. "You could lend them to me if it works," he said, "because you're not in the half-mile, and I shall need all the help I can get, if I'm not going to come in last."

"You'll need more than spikes," Jennings replied. "I can't see anything less than jet-propelled skates getting you twice round the track before it gets dark. I shouldn't be surprised if Mr Carter puts his stopwatch back in his pocket, and times you with a calendar."

Darbishire ignored the insults. "As a matter of fact," he said importantly, "I've worked out a theory that I might win, after all. My father says that when the hare and the tortoise had a race – "

"Yes, I know," Jennings broke in, "the hare went to sleep and the tortoise won. I think that's a crazy story, and if you imagine that Nuttall and Bod and Binns major are going to lie down in the middle of the running track, and have a snooze with everybody yelling their heads off, you must be bats."

He put his gym shoes on and struggled into his blazer. "Come on," he said, "let's go and have another look at the san. If only we could get in and have a good snoop round upstairs, we might be able to spot imperceptible traces."

"You think the tramps are still there, then?"

"Not in the daytime, of course. But what's to stop them getting in when the place is empty? It's just the spot for a good night's rest, and the next morning Ivy would never know they'd been there."

"She might if she went upstairs," Darbishire objected, "because if they've been sleeping there for as long as you make out, it's high time they had clean sheets, and you're not going to tell me – "

"Well, perhaps they don't bother about sheets, and if they tidy up a bit before they leave in the morning, how's the eye of the untrained observer going to find out?" It was obvious that only someone skilled in the art of deduction could detect the tell-tale traces, and Jennings was anxious to try his hand.

It was nearly a week since Venables had accidentally set the whole school talking about Jennings' discovery. As Mr Carter had prophesied, interest had waned as nothing further had happened, and everyone had dismissed the sensational news as being another of Jennings' wild-goose chases. Everyone except Jennings; he was reluctant to give up hope, and still did his best to stay awake on the chance of seeing the light again. One night he had managed to keep his eyes open till eleven-thirty, but it so happened that it was Hawkins' night off duty, and the sanatorium had remained unlighted and unswept.

They trotted across to the sanatorium and stared once more at the creeper-covered walls. Ivy was busy darning socks in her room, but she left her chair, as a laundry van crossed the quadrangle and turned into the cottage garden. The driver got down as Ivy opened the door, and after chatting for a few moments, he started to drag the heavy laundry baskets along the hall and pile them into the back of the van.

"Wait here, Darbi," whispered Jennings, "I'm going to try and fox in through the back door, while Ivy's talking to that chap at the front."

Stealthily, he made his way across the small garden which surrounded the cottage. He knew that he would not be seen so long as the maid and the vanman were busy, but time was short and he would have to hurry. He tried the back door; it was locked. What should he do? Then he remembered the sewing-room window. He had noticed that it was open when they had stood watching Ivy busy with her darning, and if the laundry man had now removed all the hampers, the room should be empty. He rounded the corner, and caught a glimpse of Darbishire standing on one leg, and twisting his fingers in an agony of guilty suspense.

The window was open at the top, and peering through he saw that the coast was clear; Ivy and the vanman must still be chatting at the front door. Carefully, Jennings raised the bottom sash, and as soon as it was wide enough to admit his slim figure, he started to crawl through, head first. Head and shoulders and the top half of his body were through the window when, suddenly, there was a jarring, shuddering noise, and the lower half of the window slid down and came gently to rest on the small of his back.

The sash cord at one side had broken months before, and the remaining cord refused to carry the extra weight. Jennings struggled, but he was unable to free himself, for the window, resting on his wriggling figure, pinned him to the sill like a botanical specimen to a drawing-board. His hands beat the empty air of the sewing-room, while his feet danced lightly in space above the flower beds outside.

He was not hurt, but the position was extremely uncomfortable; he dared not shout to Darbishire for help, for his head was the wrong side of the window, and cries for assistance would sail down the hall and be heard by Ivy at the front door.

It seemed a long time before he felt small hands clutching at his legs. At last! Darbishire had raced to the rescue. Now all would be well. It would be the work of a moment for him to raise the ill balanced sash and release his struggling friend, before the maid had noticed anything amiss.

Darbishire was not at his best in a crisis, and he was too flurried to give much thought to the best way of achieving his object. All he knew was that he must do something, and do it soon. He seized the waving ankles and tugged, in the mistaken hope that the rest of his friend would follow in the same direction.

Jennings felt the tug, and his opinion of Darbishire as a friend in need sank like a lift-shaft. "The boneheaded ruin!" he stormed to himself. "Why doesn't he lift the window up?" But though Darbishire was so close at hand, Jennings had no means of telling him what to do.

Darbishire heaved again, and Jennings lashed out wildly with his feet, as a signal that this was not the best way of effecting a rescue. "The stupid idiot," Darbishire muttered to himself, "why doesn't he keep his feet still, so's I can get a good grip!"

Battling against fearful odds, Darbishire succeeded in getting a fresh hold on the flailing legs. He tugged again. Jennings' gym shoes and ankle socks came away in his hands, and the rescuer sat down with a sudden thump amongst the delphiniums.

The door of the sewing-room opened and Ivy walked in.

"Jennings! What on earth!" she began, and then started to shriek with laughter at the legless body wriggling on the windowsill. She was still laughing when she opened the window, and helped the victim into the room.

Jennings did not laugh; it was undignified for detective-inspectors to flap helplessly in mid-air, and he felt his position keenly. He'd tell Darbishire a thing or two when he found him again!

"What's the game?" demanded Ivy. She stopped laughing and looked sternly at the barefooted figure before her. "You know you're not allowed over here. I've a good mind to report you to Mr Carter."

Jennings said nothing. There was nothing he could say.

"Playing hide-and-seek and all that carry on! And out of bounds too. You ought to be ashamed of yourself," grumbled Ivy.

Hide-and-seek! Did Sherlock Holmes ever suffer such indignities? He opened his mouth to protest and then closed it again. It was better to bear this disgrace than to embark on difficult explanations.

"You'd better make yourself useful, now you're here," said Ivy. "I've forgotten to bring Mr Wilkins' laundry over and Les Perks is here with the van. Will you take him across and show him Mr Wilkins' room for me?"

"Yes, all right," said Jennings, "and Ivy, you – er – you won't report this to Mr Carter, will you?"

"Perhaps I will, perhaps I won't." But Jennings knew by the tone in which she said it that his breaking of bounds would go no further. "She's not a bad old stick," he thought, as he led the vanman across the quadrangle.

Darbishire had disappeared, and Jennings was conscious that Mr Leslie Perks was looking at his freezing feet with some curiosity. He was a young man and he wore a chauffeur's cap; but there his attempt at a uniform stopped, for he was dressed in an old brown sports coat and dirty flannel trousers.

"Thinking of going for a paddle, son?" he inquired, as Jennings picked his way painfully over the gravel.

When they reached the main hall Jennings said: "If you go along to the end and turn left up the stairs, you'll see Mr Wilkins' room opposite."

"Okay, son," replied the vanman.

He strolled down the hall looking about him with interest, while Jennings stood on one leg and searched his smarting feet for fragments of gravel and traces of frost-bite. When he looked up again, he caught sight of the youthful Mr Perks turning right, into the library, instead of left, to mount the stairs. He scampered after him to correct the mistake, and found him standing in the middle of the library floor, admiring the trophies on the mantelpiece.

"You've gone the wrong way. You should have turned left when you got to the end," Jennings explained. "This is the library."

"Okay, son, I heard you," the man returned pleasantly. "No harm in having a look round, is there?" He walked to the door and disappeared up the stairs.

Jennings found Darbishire in the tuck-box room. He was giving his spectacles their weekly polish with a football sock, and breathing hard on the lenses to remove the sticky smears which had blurred his vision for the previous seven days.

"Oh, hallo," he said, rather sheepishly. "What happened?"

Jennings scowled.

"Darbishire, you're the world's ozardest oik. You've got no more idea of how to be a detective than a cabbage!"

"D'you mean no more idea than a cabbage has of how to be a detective, or than I have of how to be a cabbage?" Darbishire inquired earnestly.

"There was I struggling like blinko and signalling with my feet, and all you do is try and pull me in half instead of getting me free."

"Oh, sorry," Darbishire apologised. "I thought that was the idea."

"What – to pull me in half?"

"No, to get you free. But what happened when Ivy hoofed in?"

"She thought I was playing hide-and-seek and ticked me off. She didn't kick up too much of a hoo-hah, though."

Jennings sat down on a tuck-box and massaged his numbed feet. "Still, if you hadn't bished it up like that, I might have found something super important, if I'd gone upstairs. It's all your fault."

Darbishire decided to change the subject. "You know," he said, "I've been looking at that ciné camera catalogue again, and I've had a rare wheeze. You know we've got eleven and eighteenpence between us?"

"We *had* eleven and eighteenpence," corrected Jennings. "We've only got three and sevenpence now."

"Well, three and sevenpence then. It's not much, but it's something. Now, suppose we both get a pound for our birthdays and another pound for Christmas, and save up all the dosh we're given to bring back to school – why, we'd have masses in no time."

He replaced his spectacles, and found to his surprise that he could see through them fairly well. All traces of dust, jam and ink had been carefully wiped away, and only his thumb and fingerprints in the centre of each lens clouded his vision. He took the catalogue from the tuck-box and glanced longingly at the illustrations of the super de luxe model. "What about it, Jen?"

"We'd be wasting our time," his friend decided. "It would take us about a hundred years to save up ninety-five guineas. We might just as well forget the whole thing. Come on, I'm going to get changed now; my feet will need de-icing apparatus and two gallons of anti-freeze, if I don't get my socks on soon."

Although Jennings had given up hope of securing the super de luxe model, the Grossman Ciné Camera Company had not given up hope of securing J C T Jennings as a customer. In a small office, high above the steady rumble of London traffic, Mr Catchpole, the sales manager, sat staring glumly at a chart on the wall. It was a graph showing the number of cameras that his firm had sold since the beginning of the year; and the more Mr Catchpole stared, the more gloomy his expression became. The red line of the graph wobbled unsteadily through the space devoted to the sales for January and February, but when it came to the first week in March, it fell like a barometer in a thunderstorm. They had sold a mere handful of cameras since the beginning of the month, and Mr Catchpole was determined that something had got to be done. He pressed the bell on his desk, and his secretary appeared.

"Oh, Miss Haskins, bring me all the inquiries about ciné cameras we've had in the last month." He drummed his fingers on the desk impatiently, and soon Miss Haskins returned with a folder containing a bundle of letters. She stood by while Mr Catchpole thoughtfully frowned his way through the small pile. Finally, he looked up and said: "Send Mr Russell to me, at once."

Mr Russell was middle-aged, keen and alert. He was an excellent salesman and his colleagues claimed that he could sell sunshades to Eskimos and fur coats to Hottentots if he had a mind to do so.

"Sit down, Mr Russell," said the manager. "I've sent for you because things are not going too well and something has got to be done. I repeat – got...to...be...done." He emphasised each syllable with a bang on the desk.

"Quite," Mr Russell agreed.

"I've been going through these inquiries we've had lately. We've sent out dozens of catalogues and hardly anyone has written back and ordered anything. The trouble is, we're getting slack. Every inquiry should lead to a sale, if you go the right way about it."

"Quite," Mr Russell agreed. He had to sit and listen to the manager's tirade every time the sales graph took a step downwards, and he was quite used to it.

"Now, here is an example," Mr Catchpole continued, taking a letter at random from the pile and quoting: "*I am thinking of buying one of your cameras and I shall be glad if you will send me a catalogue, as advertised. Yours truly, J C T Jennings.*" He paused.

"Now, Mr Russell, what does Mr Jennings' letter suggest to you?"

"That he wants a catalogue."

"No, no, no." Mr Catchpole rose from his revolving chair and paced the office. "He's had a catalogue: we sent it weeks ago – and what's the result?"

"We hear no more," Mr Russell deduced neatly.

"Exactly, because we're not going the right way about it. We've got to be more careful with our wealthy clients. They expect the personal touch."

"Does he say he's a wealthy client?" inquired Mr Russell.

"Not in so many words, he doesn't; but reading between the lines it's obvious. Look at this." He thrust Temple's carefully written letter into Mr Russell's hand. "Look at it," he repeated. "Finest quality notepaper with *Linbury Court, Sussex*, in embossed letters. You don't call your house a Court if you live in a prefabricated bungalow! And look at the crest! And the old family motto in Latin. Do *you* have crested notepaper? No... Do *I* have crested notepaper?"

"No," said Mr Russell, supplying the expected answer.

"And why not?" But Mr Catchpole had no intention of letting his assistant work out the answer to this question for himself. "I'll tell you why not," he went on. "Because these coats-of-arms are the prorigrative – er – pogrogative – er – I should say the perigratov – "

"Prerogative," corrected Mr Russell.

"That's what I said. They are the prerogative of wealthy aristocratic families with big houses and large country estates."

Mr Catchpole warmed to his task. This Mr Jennings, he explained – he might even be Sir J C T Jennings for all they knew – was probably the squire of the village, rolling in money, and more than willing to buy expensive cameras, if he was approached in the right way.

Mr Russell was impressed with the manager's keen powers of observation and his uncanny ability to read between the lines.

"Very well, sir," he said. "I think perhaps you're right. I'll go down to Sussex one day next week and try the personal touch." He rose from his seat and made for the door.

"One moment," Mr Catchpole called him back. "I want you to understand just how important this is. If my deductions are correct, it may lead to bigger things. If this Mr Jennings buys a camera, everybody who is anybody in his part of the county will be wanting one too."

"Don't worry, sir," replied Mr Russell. "I know how to treat a man in his position. I'll find out his interests and get him talking; I dare say he'll be keen on hunting, shooting and fishing and all that. You leave it to me."

"Good," said Mr Catchpole. "I suggest you go next Wednesday, and take our latest model and plenty of film to demonstrate with."

Mr Russell's hand was on the door-knob, as the manager added good-humouredly: "And don't you dare to come back without selling a camera!"

"Trust me," grinned Mr Russell, and the door closed behind him.

Mr Catchpole smiled happily. He knew he could rely on his head salesman not to let him down.

10

Alarming Excursion

Lieut.-General Sir Melville Merridew, Bart., DSO, MC, had agreed to present the sports cup to the winning house. The news was announced at breakfast on the day before the sports, and it raised the enthusiasm of the rival houses to a simmering pitch of excitement.

They had not been expecting such an important visitor, for it was only on Speech Day, in the summer term, that the school usually welcomed distinguished Old Linburians.

Jennings spent the morning break in borrowing drawing-pins to convert his plimsoles into spiked running shoes, and Darbishire retired to the library to try to pick up a few hints from a book on athletics.

"What's so cracking wizard about it," Temple observed in the dormitory that night, "is that as it's not Speech Day, the old geezer will only have to hand over the cup and ask for a half-holiday. And that means we shan't have to sit and listen for three and a half hours while he tells us that being at school is the happiest time of your life."

"My father was asked to say a few words to the infants' school in his parish last term," said Darbishire, looking round with an important air. "He had to present the plasticine modelling prize to the *under fives*, and he told them that education was derived from the Latin word *educare*, meaning to lead out and – "

"That's just the sort of thing your father *would* say," Atkinson broke in. He was sitting on his bed, trying to lassoo his toes with his dressing-gown cord, and he had no wish to listen to the wise words of the Reverend Percival Darbishire.

"This time tomorrow," he sang out gaily, "Raleigh will have won the cup for the third time running. Super-wizzo-sonic!"

"No, they won't, then," Jennings called out from the wash-basin. "Drake will. Good old Drake. Yippee!"

Of the five boys who slept in Dormitory 4, he and Darbishire were the only members of Drake; and they were desperately keen on helping their house to wrest the challenge cup from last year's victors. "Up with Drake and down with Raleigh," he shouted, breaking off his washing operations to perform a restrained war dance round the beds.

He still carried his sponge, which dripped soddenly on to the end of each bed as he passed by, while little streams of soapy water trickled down his spine and chest until they reached the top of his pyjama trousers.

"Raleigh for ever!" called Venables, waving his toothbrush like a tomahawk.

"Good old Raleigh!" sang out Temple and Atkinson in unison.

"Good old – " Darbishire began.

"Shut up, Darbishire," the Raleigh supporters turned on him threateningly.

"Nobody asked you to butt in," Temple added. "It's just super hairy cheek for an oik who can't run for little apples to start airing his opinions like that."

"I was only going to say – 'Good old General Sir Melville Merridew for asking for a half-holiday' – just supposing that he does," Darbishire explained.

The next moment Mr Carter came in to see what all the noise was about.

"We'll win tomorrow, won't we, sir?" Jennings appealed to his house-master for support. "Raleigh won't have an earthly, will they, sir?"

"It won't be a walk-over for either side," Mr Carter replied. "It's going to be the closest competition we've had for years."

The contest was so arranged that the winners of the different events scored points for their houses, and Jennings knew that Drake was relying on him to do well in the under twelve class. "Gosh!" he said, drying his neck vigorously, "I've simply got to win the long-jump and the '440' tomorrow."

Mr Carter waited until they were all in bed; then he switched off the light.

Jennings was soon asleep. He had given up his nightly vigil of the sanatorium, and had little time to worry about the mystery, now that the inter-house sports were filling his mind and claiming his energy. And he would have continued in his deep, dreamless sleep until the shrilling of the rising bell next morning, if Mr Wilkins had not offered to help his colleague with his supervision duties.

Mr Carter made a practice of walking round all the dormitories after the boys had gone to sleep. He patrolled quietly, stopping here and there to tuck in a sliding blanket, or to straighten some fidgety sleeper who was in danger of falling out of bed. But on that Tuesday evening he was busy making final arrangements for the sports, and Mr Wilkins volunteered to see that all was well in his stead.

He set off on his round, striving to soften his usual heavy footsteps by walking on tiptoe; but he was not accustomed to this nightly patrol in the dark, and when he reached Dormitory 4, he collided heavily with the foot of a bed. The sleeper stirred, uttered a mournful moan and turned over, and

Mr Wilkins passed on, satisfied that he had not disturbed anyone's rest.

The disturbed sleeper did not, however, fall asleep again. As the piercing squeak of Mr Wilkins' tiptoeing shoes echoed down the dormitory, the drowsy figure sat up, vaguely wondering what had wakened him. There was a noisy click as Mr Wilkins closed the door with extreme care, and a heavy thump as he accidentally kicked it with his departing heels.

Jennings lay down and was about to fall asleep again, when the school clock struck eleven. As he counted the strokes, he thought of the last time he had heard this nightly chime, and he suddenly sat upright. The next moment he was at the window, shivering with excitement and staring across the deserted quadrangle. The first floor of the sanatorium was, as usual, in darkness, but a dim light was shining through the sewing-room blind.

He sped across the room to the sleeping Darbishire, and shook him.

"Darbi, wake up…wake up!"

"Uh?" grunted the sleeping Darbishire.

"Wake up, man – it's urgent."

"Wasmarrer?" came from below the sheet.

"It's me – Jennings. Are you awake?"

"I'm not sure: I think I am."

"Well, listen," Jennings hissed in an unsteady whisper. "I've seen the light."

Darbishire raised his head and blinked at the shadowy figure before him.

"You've done what?"

"I've seen the light."

"Oh, well done," said Darbishire sleepily. "I'm so glad. My father knew a man in his parish who saw the light. He became quite a reformed character in the end, but up to that time he'd been a notorious evil-doer." He closed his eyes, and settled himself down comfortably on the pillow.

"Wake up, and don't natter," whispered Jennings. "Listen – it's the tramp."

"Oh, I don't think he was a tramp," murmured Darbishire, still vague with sleep. "My father said he was a brand plucked from the burning."

"Who was?"

"The notorious evil-doer who saw the light."

Jennings shook him again. "Pull yourself together, Darbishire. There's someone in the san."

"How do you know?" yawned the bundle beneath the bedclothes.

"I've just told you. I've just – well, there's a light burning. Come on, we're going over there. Don't you understand?"

Suddenly Darbishire was wide awake and wishing that he wasn't. He understood only too well; the moment that had been such fun to talk about had become a reality. If only he could cope with these situations like the children in the library book that he was reading. They were known as the *Fearless Four*, and they excelled in this sort of adventure. They rode ponies with the skill of Middle-West cowboys; they handled sailing dinghies in rough seas like experienced yachtsmen; much of their time was spent in searching for buried treasure, which they never failed to discover every time they went for a country holiday. Dealing with tramps in empty cottages would have been meat and drink to the *Fearless Four*, but Darbishire knew that he was not cut out for such desperate action. He brought his mind back to Jennings' hair-raising invitation and swallowed hard.

"When you say we are going over there," he inquired anxiously, "do you mean – er – me, too?"

"You said you would," Jennings reminded him.

"I know I did," Darbishire admitted. "And it did seem rather a good wheeze in the daytime, but I don't think I'll bother now, if you don't mind. You see, my father says that discretion is the better part of valour, and I don't want you to think I'm trying to back out of it, but – "

"Oh, don't be a funk! All the chaps said you'd be frightened," Jennings urged, "so here's your chance to prove them wrong."

"Oh, gosh!" said Darbishire unhappily. There was no sound in the dormitory, except the rhythmic breathing of the other occupants. How he envied them! "I can't prove them wrong," he said in a cracked, unnatural voice, "because I shall still be frightened, even if I do go."

"You'll be all right," his friend assured him. "It's quite safe, really. We'll just have a quick squint to make sure it really *is* tramps, and then we'll beetle back and tell Mr Carter."

Darbishire pushed back the bedclothes and put one foot on the linoleum. "Well, no dacka-dacka stuff and pretending to take prisoners, like those gang games we used to play."

"Of course not: this isn't a game – this is the real thing."

"I know, that's the trouble," Darbishire complained as he got out of bed and fumbled for his dressing-gown. "As it isn't a game, you can't say *pax* when you've had enough."

Jennings was unable to prevent his hands from trembling as he groped beneath his bed for his shoes. He could not find his bedroom slippers, but fortunately his newly-cleaned gym shoes were under his chair, ready for the next afternoon. Quickly he slipped the first shoe on, and a strangled shriek rang out as he pressed his foot on to a drawing-pin. Then he remembered; he had converted them into spiked running shoes, and one of the spikes must have worked its way back inside. What a good thing he'd discovered it in time; supposing they had all worked through during the '440!' He removed the drawing-pins and left them on the floor, where Atkinson's bare feet discovered them the following morning.

Darbishire was looking anxious when Jennings rejoined him.

"Oughtn't we to have a weapon, or something?" he inquired. "We might be attacked."

Jennings assured him that this was most unlikely, for the purpose of their expedition was merely to spy out the lie of the land. Brave though he was, Jennings had no intention of tackling an unknown number of desperadoes. However, they decided that the feel of a weapon in their hands would be comforting, so they tiptoed out of the dormitory and made for the housemaid's cupboard on the landing.

Jennings selected a long-handled mop and Darbishire, after some thought, armed himself with the suction-hose of a vacuum cleaner.

Stealthily, they crept along the landing and past Mr Carter's room. A light shone from under the door and volcanic rumblings of conversation from within told them that Mr Wilkins was paying the housemaster a visit. This was a good thing, for Mr Wilkins' voice made a sufficient barrage of sound for the two boys to reach the head of the staircase without being heard. Cautiously they descended, crossed the main hall and slipped back the bolt of a side door which opened on to the quadrangle.

It was cold outside, but it was not only the temperature that caused Darbishire's teeth to chatter like a clicking turnstile; and after they had gone a few yards he halted uncertainly.

"Can't we go back?" he suggested.

"Gosh, no, don't be such a funk. It'll be all right," his chief assured him.

"Oh, please don't think I'm frightened: at least, not much. It's just that – er – I've got a sore place on my heel, and Matron said not to walk on it too much, if I want to be fit for the half-mile tomorrow."

"But if we go back now, we'll miss all the excitement," Jennings urged. He was not going to admit defeat now they had come so far; but Darbishire was feeling anything but eager, and said: "Well, we could still talk about it, and after all, these sort of things are miles wizarder fun to talk about than they are to do."

Jennings faced his assistant squarely. "We can't possibly go back now," he insisted. "Can't you just imagine the hoo-hah that Temple and Atkinson and everyone would kick up, if they found out that we'd seen the light, and then bished it all up because we didn't dare to follow it up? Gosh, our names would be mud with a capital M."

They walked on across the quadrangle. It was deathly quiet, save for the eerie hooting of an owl which brought Darbishire's heart into his mouth the first time he heard it. "They've seen us – they're signalling with owl noises," he gasped.

"Rats," said Jennings, "that's a proper owl. Come on, we're nearly there."

The light was clearly visible in the sewing-room window, and every step they took, the more jumpy Darbishire became. He tried to think of some comforting advice from the wise sayings of his father, but the only words which he could call to mind were about the folly of rushing headlong into danger. Jennings walked in silence, but Darbishire's nervousness took the form of a continuous stream of prattle about improbable and impossible perils which might, or might not, lie ahead.

"I feel like that chap in a poem my father made me learn," he said. "It's all about a chap *who on a lonesome road doth walk in fear and dread…*"

Jennings was not listening. "I think I can see his shadow moving on the blind," he whispered excitedly.

"*And having once looked back, walks on and turns no more his head*," Darbishire quoted.

"Ssh! We mustn't let him see us. We'll have to creep like mice."

"*Because he knows a frightful fiend doth close behind him tread*," he finished with a gulp.

Jennings' eyes were staring ahead, and his mind was but dimly aware that his friend was talking.

"What did you say, Darbi?"

"I said," Darbishire replied, "that a frightful fiend doth close behind him tread."

"Treads close behind who?"

"Anyone on a lonesome road who doth walk." Jennings glanced back the way they had come. What was that strange white figure lurking on the rugger pitch? He breathed again, as he recognised it as a goal post.

"I can't see anyone treading behind us," he said uneasily.

"Of course you can't – there's no one there."

"You said there was."

"No, I didn't. I said the chap in the poem thought there was, so having once looked back, he walked on and turned no more his head."

Jennings was tempted to knock his assistant over the head with his mop.

"You ancient, prehistoric remains, Darbi!" he jerked out in a hoarse, voiceless whisper. "Here we are, bang up to the eyebrows in the most supersonic hoo-hah we've ever struck, and you have to start reciting poetry."

"Sorry, Jen," Darbishire whispered humbly.

They crept on, and a moment later they reached the small garden. Jennings had no clear idea of what he was going to do next. Had he been able to see his quarry through the window, he would have considered that to be sufficient evidence, and returned to school for help. Unfortunately the blind was down and he could see no one, and with some misgiving he decided that they would have to go in. They made a circuit of the garden, and when they reached the back of the building, Jennings gripped his companion's arm.

"The back door's open. That means I shan't have to use my skeleton key, after all."

"I didn't know you'd got one."

"Well, it's my tuck-box key really," Jennings explained, "but it fits the stationery cupboard and the music room, so it would probably open anything in an emergency. Ssh! Come on."

"Just a minute."

"What is it now?"

"Well, we've neither of us got our special secret Linbury Detective Agency badges on. Don't you think we ought to go back for them?"

"No, I don't! And anyway, we're not going to get close enough for anyone to read them, if I can help it."

Holding their weapons poised, they tiptoed through the back door into the kitchen, where they stood for a moment, straining their ears to catch the tell-tale sound of an intruder. They could hear nothing except their own heavy breathing, though they were both conscious of the loud pounding of their hearts.

With mop upraised, Jennings took a step forward, and suddenly froze in his tracks. Thin rays of moonlight shining through the uncurtained window revealed an unnerving glimpse of a shadowy figure not two feet away. The figure held a stick and stood ready to strike.

"Oooh!" Jennings gasped, and sprang sideways to dodge the threatened blow. But the blow did not fall; and when he glanced quickly in the direction of his assailant, he understood the reason. He had been standing in front of a large mirror screwed to the kitchen wall, and the shadowy figure with upraised stick had been J C T Jennings with his mop at the ready. He breathed again and looked round. Darbishire had disappeared.

"Darbi!" he whispered softly. "Where are you?"

A breathless squeak from beneath the kitchen table told that his assistant had taken cover at the first sound of his chief's startled gasp. Somewhat shaken, he emerged, and together they tiptoed to the door leading into the hall. All was quiet.

Jennings said "Ssh!" and cautiously turned the knob and opened the door a few inches.

The hall was dark, but the light was still shining from beneath the sewing-room door and, as they, listened, they could hear faint sounds coming from within. They advanced a few paces, and then came to an uncertain halt.

"Ssh! There's someone there," Jennings whispered. "He's moving about. Ssh!"

"D-don't keep saying Ssh!" Darbishire whispered back. "It m-makes more r-row than not sh-shushing at all."

"Sounds as though he's moving the furniture," Jennings observed in an undertone, as a low scraping noise became audible.

"Come on, let's g-go then. We've got to tell Mr Carter."

"Okay. I wish you'd stop your teeth chattering. You sound like a tap dancer."

"I've got the w-wind up," Darbishire admitted. "My heart's beating like a s-sledge-hammer."

Jennings decided to retreat. They had not actually seen their man, but they knew beyond all doubt that he was there.

"Right then, we'll slip out the way we came in, and dash straight back and tell Mr Carter."

He turned to lead the way back to the kitchen, and in the darkness he bumped into Darbishire who was standing close behind him. Darbishire dropped the vacuum cleaner suction-hose in his agitation and Jennings, slightly off his balance, tripped over it and crashed to the floor.

He lay where he fell, not daring to breathe, and it was as much as Darbishire could do to stop himself from shouting for help; for immediately the scraping noise in the sewing-room ceased, and a second later the light clicked off. Then the door swung open, and footsteps were coming towards them along the darkened hall.

11

Mr Wilkins Answers the Phone

"Quick!" yelled Jennings, as all need for caution was now over. "Get back into the kitchen!"

But as he scrambled to his feet, he was blinded by a powerful beam of torchlight shining in his eyes, and before they could find the kitchen door, their unknown adversary had rushed up and seized Darbishire by the arm.

Jennings saw the torch waving wildly, as the man sought to hold Darbishire, and he brought his long-handled mop down with a crashing blow on what he hoped was the tramp's head: but the dazzling light in his eyes spoiled all chance of a straight aim, and his mop cut through empty air. The next moment the torch went out, and he felt a strong hand grabbing at his arm.

"Let me go," Jennings shouted; "take your hands off me!"

"You keep quiet," came a low, gruff voice, from just above his head. "We don't want no more of that shouting."

Darbishire emitted a voiceless "H-h-help!" which died at once, as their assailant clapped a hand over his mouth. Struggling and squirming, the two boys were dragged across the hall to the door which stood opposite the kitchen. It opened, under pressure of a kick from their captor's foot, and they were roughly bundled inside.

The gruff voice spoke again. "You get in 'ere, both of you, and stop that row. If you make a sound you'll cop it."

He shut the door and turned the key, and the boys could hear his footsteps crossing the hall, and retreating through the kitchen, and out of the back door.

Jennings was the first to find his voice. "Are you all right, Darbi?" he gasped.

"I... I...think so," came out of the empty blackness in the middle of the room. "But, oh, golly!"

Darbishire felt once again that he was not keeping up the standard of cool daring which the children in his library book would have expected of him. *The Fearless Four* often met sinister assailants in darkened passages, and had no difficulty in getting the better of them, and tying them up with lengths of strong twine, which, by chance they always had in their pockets.

But not Charles Edwin Jeremy Darbishire! He knew that he would never be capable of such feats, even if his pockets were bulging with strong twine. He stood breathing heavily in the middle of the room, while he fumbled to replace his spectacles. They had suffered during the encounter, and now hung from one ear with the lenses dangling below his chin.

Jennings leapt at once into action. He found the light switch by the door, and they stood blinking, as the room was flooded with light.

"Where are we?" asked Darbishire, peering round short-sightedly.

"We're in the room that the night nurse uses when there's somebody ill," Jennings explained, and his eyes shone with excitement. "And look, Darbi, I've got a valuable clue."

"What?"

Jennings opened his clenched fist and revealed a small, brown sleeve button. "I got hold of his arm and it came off," he exclaimed in triumph.

"You mean he'd got a false arm?"

"No, you goof. The button came off. Gosh, I bet the police will say it's a wizard clue. Come on, we've got to get out, quick."

"Oh, gosh! Have we got to chase him, and start that struggling business all over again?" asked, Darbishire, appalled.

"We don't want him to make a getaway, do we?"

"I do. The farther the getaway the better. I'll shout for help if you like, though."

"Fat lot of good that would be. No one would ever hear you."

Jennings tried the door, and then rushed to the window; but it was blocked by a large mirror, forming part of a heavy dressing-table. By the time they had moved it, their enemy would be far away. Quickly, he glanced round the room, seeking other methods of escape. Then suddenly, he shouted "Look, Darbi, look over there!"

Darbishire looked round vaguely. "I can't see very well," he mumbled. "My teeth are still chattering."

"You don't see with your teeth, do you?"

"No, but I'm still suffering from tremble-itis, and I can't put my glasses on properly."

In two bounds Jennings crossed the room, and stopped before a small table in a far corner. On the table was a telephone.

"Super-duper-sonic," he cried. "We're saved, Darbi! We can phone the police and get them to send a flying squad. It'll be miles quicker than getting through the window, and going all the way back for Mr Carter."

He grabbed the receiver and put it to his ear. "Oh, golly, I don't know what the number is."

"That doesn't matter," said Darbishire. "You just ask for Ambulance or Police. And when you get the police, it might be a good wheeze to ask for an ambulance as well, just in case we meet that chap again."

"The exchange are a jolly long time answering," Jennings complained. "Either that, or the line's dead. There's no buzzing, or clicking, or burring, or anything going on. Of course, if that chap was a burglar and not just a tramp, he might have cut the telephone wires, mightn't he?"

"Give them a bit longer," Darbishire urged. "After all, they're probably in bed, and they've got to get up and find their dressing-gowns and slippers and things."

"But dash it all, this is urgent. All the time they're crawling about looking for their slippers, our burglar is getting farther and farther away."

He jogged the receiver-rest up and down and fidgeted with impatience. Opening his clenched fist he looked again at the intruder's sleeve button. He must be careful; there might be fingerprints on it, he decided. In point of fact there were, but the prints were those of J C T Jennings.

He slipped the button into his dressing-gown pocket, intending to hand this valuable clue to the police. What on earth was the matter with the telephone exchange? Surely they were not still looking for their slippers?

Then he noticed a small brown box with a handle, standing next to the telephone. It was a generator, and as the sanatorium was only an extension of the main telephone line, it was necessary to turn the handle before the instrument could be used.

It was Darbishire who discovered this first. "Look," he said, "I think I know what's wrong. My father once explained how the telephone works. Try putting the receiver back, and turning this handle thing first."

Jennings did so.

"That's right," said Darbishire. "You'll be through in no time now."

In one respect Darbishire was right. The wire hummed, and a few moments later a voice answered. But the line was not switched through to the exchange as the boys supposed: it was, instead, connected with the telephone in Mr Carter's study.

Mr Wilkins broke off in the middle of a sentence, when the telephone rang.

"That's odd!" he exclaimed. "Who on earth is ringing us up at this time of the night? Hope it's not General Merridew to say he can't come."

Mr Carter looked up from the sports list he was checking. "It can't be," he replied. "That's not the exchange – it's one of the extension lines. Probably the Head to tell me – " He broke off, and narrowed his brows in a puzzled frown. "No, it can't be the Head either. This call is coming from the sanatorium."

Mr Carter was usually at home in the evenings, and for this reason the small switchboard was situated in his room. He could switch incoming calls through to the Headmaster's study, or the sanatorium, and anyone wishing to speak from either of these places had to contact Mr Carter before they could be put through to the exchange.

"The sanatorium!" echoed Mr Wilkins in surprise. "But there's nobody there, except Old Nightie, propping himself up with a broom-handle. He's not likely to – "

"Wouldn't it be better to answer the phone and find out," his colleague broke in, as the bell sounded again. "Much more satisfactory than playing guessing games."

Mr Wilkins snatched the receiver from its rest. "Hallo," he said.

A high-pitched, excited voice at the other end of the line said: "Is that the exchange? I want the police station, please – it's urgent. There's been a burglary at Linbury Court School with assault and battery, and another boy and I have been locked in, and we want the police to send a flying squad."

"Hold on a moment," said Mr Wilkins, taking the receiver from his ear; he clapped his hand over the mouthpiece and his face turned a deep purple, as he struggled to stifle the laughter that was shaking his powerful frame like a pneumatic drill.

Mr Carter raised his eyebrows. "What's the joke?"

For a moment Mr Wilkins was unable to speak, and then with an effort he controlled himself, and sank his loud voice to a whisper. "It's Jennings," he croaked, voicelessly. "They've gone over to the san and Old Nightie has collared them and locked them in. That ought to cool their hot heads for them!" His shoulders heaved and his hands shook. When Mr Wilkins thought that something was funny, the matter could never be kept quiet.

Mr Carter threw down his pencil in annoyance. "Silly little idiots," he muttered. "I wish to goodness I'd had them up here and dispelled all this burglary nonsense at the start."

It was, he felt, largely his fault; but he had been so certain that the sanatorium expedition would never come to anything, that he had decided to let the excitement die a natural death. Nine times out of ten this would have been the right course to adopt – but this was the tenth time, and he had not reckoned with Jennings' single-tracked keenness for the job on hand.

"It's all right," Mr Wilkins whispered. "Nothing to worry about. It'll do them far more good than a lecture from you. If Old Nightie has given them a bit of a scare, they won't be so eager to try these capers any more. He'll probably be up in a moment to tell us he's bagged a couple of very worried detectives."

A shrill voice could be heard buzzing indistinctly from the other end of the line. Mr Wilkins removed his hand from the mouthpiece and listened. Then in an assumed voice he said: "One moment, please. I'm trying to connect you."

Mr Carter stared at him in astonishment. He was preparing to start for the sanatorium at once, but Mr Wilkins signalled to him to stop. Covering the mouthpiece once more, he said: "Wait till Old Nightie comes across; he won't be long."

"Why bother to wait? Those boys ought to be – "

"Yes, I know," Mr Wilkins broke in. "But let's finish the joke first."

His face turned a deeper shade of purple as he savoured the humour of the situation to the full. "It's no good, Carter," he went on. "I can't resist the temptation. I've always wanted to be a policeman." And to Mr Carter's shocked surprise, he spoke into the instrument in a heavily disguised voice. "Hallo," he said. "Police Station here. Sergeant Snodgrass speaking."

"Oh, thank goodness," came the voice from the other end of the wire. "You've been ages. I'm so afraid it'll be too late."

The voice launched into an involved stream of explanation, while the bogus Sergeant Snodgrass sat and rocked in silent mirth, and Mr Carter wondered why fate had given him a colleague who enjoyed such a puerile sense of humour.

" 'Ere, 'ere, 'ere, not so fast," rumbled the self-appointed sergeant. "So you've had a burglar, eh! Well, fancy that now. You're sure he was a burglar, I suppose, and not just a chap who'd come in out of the rain?"

"Of course I'm sure," replied Jennings. "Besides, it's not raining."

"Well, well, so it isn't; I never noticed. Smart of you to spot that. You'd make a good detective you would," said the sergeant admiringly, and Jennings was too agitated to detect anything unusual in Sergeant Snodgrass' methods of coping with urgent cases of housebreaking. Neither did he pause to wonder why a Sussex policeman should have a strong Lancashire accent.

"Oh, do hurry up," he said. "We're locked in the sanatorium, and we can't do anything until you send a flying squad."

"Locked you in, eh! Tut, tut, tut, that's bad! The larks these burglars get up to. Well, I never did!" Mr Wilkins was enjoying himself. He was very pleased with his impersonation, and was unmindful of the fact that the East Sussex Constabulary would have been horrified had they known that such a travesty was being carried out in their name. "Yes, but if I come round to a sanatorium," the flat Lancashire accent dragged on, "I'd be more likely to catch measles than burglars."

Mr Carter raised despairing eyes to the ceiling, and wondered how much longer his colleague intended to indulge in Third Form humour. He fidgeted impatiently as the conversation went on.

"Then what was he doing in a sanatorium if he wasn't ill?" Mr Wilkins inquired heavily, and after a babble of explanation from the other end, he said: "Ah, maybe he wasn't when he first went in, but he's bound to have caught something by this time."

Jennings could hardly believe his ears. That a member of the police force, and a sergeant at that, should talk in such a ridiculous manner was more than he could understand. "Look here," he said, "are you going to send a flying squad, or aren't you? Because I've jolly well had enough of these questions."

Mr Carter tapped his colleague on the shoulder as a sign that this nonsense had gone quite far enough, and Mr Wilkins rang off, after promising to investigate the matter the next time he happened to be passing. Then he sat back in his chair and roared with laughter.

"They'll feel so silly when they find out it was Old Nightie who locked them in," he gasped.

"Come on," said Mr Carter. "Hawkins doesn't seem to be coming over, so we'd better go and let them out."

Together they went down the stairs, and as they reached the hall they heard the sound of footsteps coming up the lower flight of steps from the basement.

Old Nightie, with mop and bucket, came into view and wished them "Good evening."

"Good evening, Hawkins," Mr Carter replied. "I gather you've got two boys safely in your care."

Old Nightie looked surprised. "No, sir," he said. "I haven't got no boys, nowhere."

"In the sanatorium, I mean," Mr Carter explained. "The two boys who came over while you were cleaning up."

The expression on the night watchman's face grew more mystified. "No, sir," he said. "I've not been over to the sanatorium yet; I'm just going now."

"What!" shouted Mr Wilkins. "You – you – you mean you've not locked any boys in?"

"No, sir. I got held up, cleaning out the clinker, down in the boiler-room. First time for years I've been late in sweeping out the san. Ten forty-five as regular as clockwork, bar tonight."

"But if you haven't been over there – " Mr Wilkins began, and broke off, unable to make sense of it all.

"It's all right, Mr Wilkins, I'm going now," Hawkins replied. "I've got me key and I'll get finished there by half-past twelve, if I get a move on." He was rather upset that, for once, his record for punctuality had been spoiled. "If it hadn't been for cleaning out the clinker in the boiler – "

"I don't understand this," Mr Carter broke in, and turning to his colleague he asked: "Wilkins, didn't Jennings tell you he'd been locked in?"

"Yes, he said they'd met a burglar. I took it for granted it was Old Ni – I beg your pardon, Hawkins, I mean I thought it was you."

"Couldn't very well have been me, could it?" Hawkins answered, "seeing as I was down the stokehold cleaning out the clinker in the boiler. First time I've been late these – "

Mr Carter spoke sternly. "Come along, we're going over there, at once. I don't like the sound of this, at all."

He led the way at a brisk pace and Mr Wilkins sprinted behind him. Old Nightie, still muttering about cleaning clinker out of boilers, hobbled after them, as fast as his flat feet would permit.

12

The Empty Mantelpiece

As they ran, Mr Carter delivered himself of a few curt remarks. "Really, Wilkins, I think you might have found out what had been going on over there, instead of playing the goat on the telephone like that. Sergeant Snodgrass indeed – what nonsense you talk!"

"Sorry, old man," panted the ex-sergeant, "but if you'd put your foot down a week earlier, this would never have happened."

"I know all about that," Mr Carter answered. He was distinctly worried, and blamed his own error of judgment for the unexpected turn that events had taken. "Can't you run any faster?" he asked irritably.

"I… I… Corwumph! Give me a chance, old man," said Mr Wilkins. "I may be ten years younger than you, but I'm thirty-eight round the middle, don't forget."

Soon they reached the small garden that surrounded the cottage. There they paused, and Mr Wilkins remarked that if there really was a burglar, he might still be lurking about in the bushes, and the best thing to do would be to have a good look round before going in.

"The boys' safety is the important thing," Mr Carter reminded him.

"They'll be all right for a minute. They're shut up in the nurse's bedroom, so they won't come to much harm."

The next moment, he seized the house-master's arm and dragged him into the cover of the hedge. "Ssh! I thought I saw someone," he whispered.

For some seconds the two men stood motionless; then Mr Wilkins stiffened. Footsteps were approaching round the corner from the back of the building, and a moment later a shadowy figure appeared on the path in front of them. The figure paused uncertainly. Judging his distance, Mr Wilkins hurled himself forward in a brilliant rugger tackle, which took his opponent just above the knees and felled him to the soft earth of the flowerbed. A moment later as he was trying to pinion the flailing arms, a shaft of moonlight lit up the frightened features of his adversary. Mr Wilkins' jaw dropped slightly.

"Oh, good heavens," he gasped. "I'm terribly sorry, Hawkins. I didn't know it was you."

He helped the night watchman to his feet, as Mr Carter joined him.

"Well, really, Wilkins," he exclaimed, "what on earth are you playing at now?"

"It was just a mistake. I heard footsteps, so I jumped. I'd no idea Hawkins had followed us over. Sorry, Hawkins – I didn't hurt you, did I?"

Old Nightie gave Mr Wilkins one of his queer looks. He was not hurt, but night watchmen as a class, are never very pleased at being brought down by low rugger tackles, when on duty.

"I came over as fast as I could. I couldn't see no sign of anybody, so I went round the other way, to see where you'd got to. Of course, if I'd known as people was going to start jumping out of bushes – " He left the sentence unfinished, but Mr Wilkins had the feeling that his name was now bracketed with the clinker in the boiler, as being the chief cause of Old Nightie's troubles.

Mr Carter decided to waste no more time. If a burglar had been lurking about before, he certainly would not be there after all the noise of the last few minutes.

The night watchman's key was not needed, for the back door was still open and the three men hurried through.

Mr Wilkins dashed into the hall and switched on the light. "That's where they are!" he cried, pointing to the night nurse's room.

Jennings and Darbishire recognised the voice.

"Gosh, it's Old Wilkie!" Jennings exclaimed in surprise. "He's got here before the police. Wonder how he knew we were over here." Raising his voice, he shouted: "We're in here, sir, and the door's locked."

"I'm coming," called Mr Wilkins. "Stand back, Hawkins, I'm going to break the door down." He took a deep breath and prepared to hurl the whole of his thirteen stone six in a thunderous shoulder-charge on the door panels.

Mr Carter stopped him.

"The fact that Jennings can't open the door from within," he said quietly, "is no reason why we should smash the place up." And he pointed to the key, which the intruder had left in the lock.

"Sorry, old man," apologised Mr Wilkins. "I didn't bother to look."

He unlocked the door and the two masters hurried in, leaving Hawkins to make a tour of the building and estimate the extent of the burglary.

"Oh, sir, I'm ever so glad you've come, sir," a rather chastened Jennings confided to his house-master. "There's been a burglary, sir."

"Yes, I know – he's got away, I'm afraid. Are both you boys all right?"

"We're all right, sir, honestly," Jennings answered, and Darbishire added: "I'm feeling just a bit shaken up, sir, but I'm very well, thank you, considering."

"Thank goodness," Mr Carter sighed with relief. "I was very worried about you."

Jennings was touched; he had no idea that masters possessed such human feelings about the boys in their care. On the other hand, of course, awkward questions and unpleasant punishments were certain to be the next item on the evening's programme, when once the excitement of liberation was over, so perhaps it would be as well not to stress their fitness too strongly.

"When I say we're all right, sir," he amended, "I mean I shouldn't be surprised if we weren't both suffering from shock. So don't you think it might be a good idea if we were to take things quietly in class for the next few days, sir?"

"It'd be a change, anyway," said Mr Wilkins. "It's not often you're quiet in my class."

"I didn't exactly mean that, sir. I meant it might be a good plan not to overdo things by working too hard and straining ourselves."

"That," said Mr Carter, "would not be a change. Come along, if you're all right. You'd better be getting back to bed. It's too late now to discuss why you stupid little boys came over here – that'll keep until the morning."

"Oh, but sir, I know we're out of bounds, sir, but it was a good job we were, wasn't it? Otherwise, sir, you wouldn't have known about the burglar, would you?"

"Never mind about the burglar," said Mr Carter sharply. "That's for me to worry about."

It was odd, he reflected, that for so many years Hawkins had arrived to clean the sanatorium punctually at ten forty-five, and in all that time nothing out of the ordinary had ever disturbed the routine of his work. "Isn't it just like Jennings," he murmured to Mr Wilkins. "The one and only time we have a burglar, and the one and only time Hawkins is late – and Jennings has to choose this night, of all nights, to come gallivanting over here."

As they were making for the door, Old Nightie appeared and reported that the cottage showed no sign of having been burgled.

Mr Carter stopped, and looked at Jennings inquiringly.

"Oh, yes, sir, there was a burglar here, all right," the boy insisted. "Wasn't there, Darbishire?"

"I think so," Darbishire replied. "Of course, it was dark and I've never actually met a burglar before, except the man my father knew who saw the light, and he was only a brand plucked from the burning – so he probably wouldn't count, would he, sir?"

"You come and see for yourself, sir," Old Nightie said. "The whole place is in apple-pie order. There's no sign of anyone breaking in – bar the back door being open." He cast one of his queer looks in the boys' direction and added meaningly: "And these two boys could have done that when they come in."

"I believe you're right, Hawkins," Mr Wilkins exclaimed, and turning to Jennings, he boomed: "Now, look here, if this is all some practical joke, you're going to find yourselves in very serious trouble."

"Oh, but, sir, honestly," protested Jennings, almost tearful that his story was not being believed. "We did meet a burglar, really. Look, sir, I've got a clue," and he produced the sleeve button for their inspection.

Mr Wilkins refused to accept this as evidence. He pointed out that lots of people lose sleeve buttons, and in any case they were next door to the sewing-room where buttons were as plentiful as pebbles on the beach.

"There's one point you're overlooking," Mr Carter broke in. "Did Jennings and Darbishire lock themselves in and leave the key on the outside?" He crossed to the window and ran his finger along the dusty ledge. "And they didn't come in this way, judging by the dust."

Old Nightie looked away uncomfortably – he did not like people examining his handiwork too closely.

Jennings slipped the button into the pocket of his pyjama jacket as Mr Carter turned towards him with a reassuring smile. "It's all right, Jennings. I don't want you to imagine for one moment that I'm doubting your word. I make it a rule never to do that." His smile broadened: "I just wanted to show you that I've learnt a thing or two from Sherlock Holmes, as well."

They left Hawkins settling down to his labours, and set off across the quadrangle. Mr Carter was anxious to get Jennings and Darbishire back to bed as soon as possible. He would have to report the matter to the Headmaster, of course, and then the police would have to be told; though it was doubtful whether they could track a criminal who had stolen nothing, and had left so little evidence of his visit. In fact, had it not been for Jennings' interference, they might never have known that a burglar had been on the premises at all. Mr Carter wondered how the Headmaster would deal with the matter; breaking bounds was a serious business, even though it was done with the best of intentions.

They crossed the quadrangle in silence, and entered the hall of the main building. Then Mr Carter said: "Go to bed, you two. I'm going upstairs to phone the police."

"Oh, but sir, I've done that already!" Jennings exclaimed. "They've promised to send a flying squad. I can't think why they're not here already."

For a moment, a smile flickered across Mr Carter's worried features. "I can," he said; "can't you, Mr Wilkins?"

Mr Wilkins studied his fingernails with great interest, and said nothing.

"The sergeant said he'd see to it, but he sounded a very stupid sort of man, sir. He seemed to think it was funny."

Mr Wilkins' interest in his fingernails became deeper, as Jennings went on: "Binns minor would have made a better policeman than the man I talked to, sir. He'd got no sense at all."

"Fancy!" said Mr Carter. "What do you make of that, Mr Wilkins?"

"All right, all right. I… I… I… Corwumph!" Mr Wilkins said hurriedly. "It's time these silly little boys were in bed."

Jennings and Darbishire went upstairs, and the two masters made for the Headmaster's private quarters at the other end of the building.

"I hope he deals with them pretty drastically," Mr Wilkins remarked. "All that fuss and nonsense, and chasing about for nothing."

"Well, they did find a burglar," Mr Carter reminded him. "I admit it was a thousand to one chance, but – "

"Burglar!" Mr Wilkins snorted. "I don't believe there was a burglar at all. It was just Jennings' vivid imagination getting the better of him. Dash it all, if anyone had really broken in, he would have stolen something, and it's quite obvious that nothing's been touched."

As they passed the library, they felt a strong draught blowing through the open door. "Old Nightie has forgotten to close the windows," Mr Carter remarked. "He must be having rather a tiresome night, what with cleaning out clinker and warding off rugger tackles."

He walked into the library and switched on the light. Fluttering curtains told of a wide-open window, but it was not this that halted Mr Carter in his tracks. Instead, he stood staring at the mantelpiece which should have held a row of gleaming silver cups.

But the mantelpiece was empty.

M W B Pemberton-Oakes, Esq., Headmaster, was not pleased when a loud banging on his bedroom door woke him from sleep. There was only one member of his staff who could make so much noise, and he had no difficulty in deducing that Mr Wilkins wished to speak to him.

It was shortly after midnight, and the Headmaster was tight-lipped with exasperation, as he rose from his bed and prepared to deal with his volcanic assistant. If Wilkins had disturbed him because of some trifling matter that could well have waited until the morning, Mr Pemberton-Oakes was prepared to be very terse indeed. He remembered an occasion, not long since, when his assistant had arrived, late at night, to report that the scullery had been struck by lightning; and investigation had shown that the trouble had been caused by the housekeeper's cat knocking down a nest of saucepans.

"Well, Wilkins, what is it?" the dressing-gowned figure of the Headmaster inquired coldly.

"There's been a burglary, sir. The cups have been stolen from the library."

"What?... And the Merridew Sports Cup as well?"

"Yes, that's gone, too. The thief got in through the window. I think you'd better come along, sir."

The Headmaster hastened down to investigate, and found Mr Carter in charge. He had telephoned for the police, and soon the wheels of a police car scrunched on the gravel, and came to rest outside the front door.

Sergeant Hutchinson, of the East Sussex Constabulary, had little in common with the mythical Sergeant Snodgrass. He was alert and business-like, as he listened to Mr Carter's summary of the events of the evening. Occasionally he asked a question, and Mr Wilkins grew hot and cold with embarrassment at the thought of having to explain his impersonation of Sergeant Snodgrass to this cool and efficient representative of the police; he was repentant, now that the incident had ceased to be funny, and he hoped that Sergeant Hutchinson would not show too much interest in the actual words of the telephone conversation.

Hawkins was sent for and confirmed that, apart from the silver cups in the library, nothing else had been taken, and there was no sign of disorder.

The Headmaster rose from his chair at the library table and paced the long length of the room. "What I am at a loss to understand," he said, "is why this midnight intruder, having stolen the athletic trophies, should go to the sanatorium at all." He gazed pensively at the chandelier, as though expecting its bright beams to shed light upon the mystery.

"I think it happened the other way round," Mr Carter suggested. "He found nothing worth taking at the cottage, so he came over here and found his luck was in."

Sergeant Hutchinson looked up from his notebook and said: "With your permission, I should like to have a word with the two boys you spoke about."

"I think it would be better if you were to interrogate them in the morning," the Headmaster replied, as he returned to his chair. "Don't you think so, Carter?"

"I certainly do," the house-master agreed. "Jennings and Darbishire have had more than enough excitement for one night."

It was nearly two o'clock in the morning when Mr Carter made his final inspection of the dormitories. Sergeant Hutchinson had completed his first examination of the premises and had driven away, promising to return as soon as it was light. The Headmaster had gone back to bed, distressed beyond measure at the thought of General Merridew arriving to present a trophy that was no longer there to present.

Mr Wilkins, also, had retired to his room; and Matron, on the floor below, had her slumbers disturbed as thuds from above announced that the former Sergeant Snodgrass was taking his shoes off, and preparing for bed. Old Nightie had gone to earth in the depths of the boiler-room, where he sat sipping a cup of cocoa, and casting reproachful glances at the heap of clinker that had contributed so much to the evening's disaster.

All was quiet in the dormitories, as Mr Carter padded noiselessly along the rows of beds. In Dormitory 4, he stopped first before the curled-up bundle that was Darbishire, snuggling beneath the bedclothes. The only things visible were a strand of light curly hair straying across the pillow, and the tip of a nose which twitched like a rabbit's, whenever it felt the tickle of the fleecy blanket.

Mr Carter crossed to Jennings' bed, missing the upturned drawing-pins by inches. Jennings was asleep too, but as Mr Carter watched, the boy's eyes opened for a moment, and he smiled as he recognised the house-master at his bedside. "Oh, sir, wasn't it smashing!" he said, and promptly fell asleep again.

13

Alibi for Old Nightie

The streaks of sunshine smiled feebly through the gaps in the billowing March clouds. They filtered gingerly through the struts of the toothbrush rack, and danced like timid ballerinas on Venables' sleeping eyelids. He awoke, and lay still for a moment, collecting his thoughts. Then he yelled "Yippee!" with a blood-curdling howl that roused the sleepers of Dormitory 4 far more effectively than the rising bell, which sounded at the same moment.

"Sports today!" sang out Venables joyfully. "On your marks…! Get set…! Wham!"

Sitting up in bed, he mimed the actions of a hundred-yard sprint as well as his restricted position would allow. His arms beat back and forth across his chest like the pistons of a reciprocating pump, as he hurtled along an imaginary race track at Olympic speed. Snorts, grunts and whistles through his clenched teeth showed the severe strain to which he was being subjected. He increased his speed for a final spurt, and the impetus sent his bed rolling gently on its castors across the linoleum.

"Gosh," exclaimed Atkinson, "how wizard! Come on, let's have a jet-propelled bedstead race."

He shook himself backwards and forwards with the energy of a small dynamo, and soon his bed was slithering across the dormitory floor in jerky pursuit. Inch by inch the intrepid drivers urged their vehicles towards the wash-basins; and Venables was within a hand's-breadth of victory, when a violent backward swing of his elbow hit the bed-rail behind his hunched shoulders, and he retired from the race considerably shaken. Atkinson vibrated the protesting castors to the finishing post, and leapt to the floor with a triumphant bound.

It was then that he discovered the drawing-pins, and the next few minutes were loud with the groans of both competitors.

"I say, you chaps," Jennings announced loudly, when the noise had died away. "Something spivish rare happened last night when you were all snoring. Darbishire and I went over to the san and caught a burglar."

Venables, Temple and Atkinson stared at him in amazement.

"You did what?" gasped Temple.

"We caught a burglar. Didn't we, Darbi?"

"Well, actually, the burglar caught us," Darbishire corrected, and shivered slightly at the memory.

"Yes, it was super-duper-sonic. I saw the light again, you see, so I woke Darbi and he nipped out of bed like lightning, and we ankled over to the san, hot-foot on the trail."

Jennings had the full attention of his gaping audience; he pressed on, carefully editing the story, and hurrying over the parts which he thought it wisest not to dwell upon in detail.

"We armed ourselves with vacuum cleaners and things, and crept in and spied on him, just like Sherlock Holmes. Gosh, it was exciting! Then Darbishire tripped me up, and there was a struggle and I caught hold of his sleeve button."

"What on earth did you want to start fighting Darbishire for?" Temple asked incredulously.

"I didn't. It was the burglar who started it."

"You said Darbishire did. You said he tripped you up."

"That was an accident. Anyway, after I got his sleeve button – "

"Whose – Darbishire's?"

"No, not Darbishire's. He was wearing his dressing-gown – I meant the burglar's. Besides, his spectacles had come off – "

"Whose – the burglar's?"

"No – Darbishire's. Why don't you listen properly?" urged the exasperated story-teller. "Anyway, we were overpowered in the end, and he locked us in a room and I telephoned for the police."

"And did they come?"

"Well, no, as a matter of fact, they didn't. But Mr Carter and Old Wilkie came instead."

Jennings was beginning to feel that he was not telling the story very well. The first gasp of astonishment had died away under Temple's cross-examination, and Jennings was aware that his audience was regarding him with suspicion.

"But if this chap locked you in," Temple persisted, "how did you get out to go and telephone?"

"There happened to be a telephone in the room."

Temple smiled meaningly, and looked at the others. "A likely story!" his raised eyebrows seemed to be saying.

"What happened to the burglar?" asked Venables. "Did you catch him?"

"No, he got away."

"What did he steal?" Atkinson demanded.

"Well, actually, he didn't steal anything, because Old Nightie came over and had a look."

Venables, Temple and Atkinson stared, hostile with disbelief, and Jennings pointed to his assistant. "You ask Darbi, then. He was there so he ought to know. And you all said he'd be frightened to go, and he wasn't, were you, Darbi?"

"Well," said Darbishire, "my father says that courage in adversity is a quality, which can only be – "

"Rats!" shouted Temple. "I don't believe a word of it. I bet you've made it all up."

"No, I haven't, I tell you."

"Prove it, then."

"Okay," said Jennings. "I'll show you the button I pulled off his cuff."

He plunged his hand into his dressing-gown pocket; then, anxiously, into the other pocket. He fumbled and felt and nearly pulled the pockets off the dressing-gown, but it was all to no purpose. The vital clue was missing.

"I know I put it in my dressing-gown," he muttered worriedly. "I can remember doing it, when I was waiting for the telephone exchange to wake up. You saw me, didn't you, Darbi?"

"Yes, it was just before I told you to turn that handle thing."

"Oh, gosh! It must have dropped out, somehow."

Temple, Atkinson and Venables hooted with derision.

"I know what it is," Atkinson explained knowingly. "They made such a hoo-hah about the detective agency and seeing the light, that they reckon they've just *got* to pretend something happened, so's we'll be impressed." He turned away and carefully eased his socks on to his injured feet.

"It's just like last time," said Venables, "when they thought they'd got a burglar, and it turned out to be the chap who puts the names on the cups. I bet they didn't really meet anyone at all. I bet they didn't even go over there."

The door opened and Mr Carter walked in; he could sense the heavy atmosphere of suspicion that lay over the room.

"Good morning, sir," came from five voices.

"Good morning."

"Sir, please sir," Temple announced. "Jennings said we had a burglar last night. He's quite mad, isn't he, sir?" And he smiled pityingly at his room-mate's mental decay.

"And he said the burglar didn't steal anything, sir," Venables added.

"I'm afraid Jennings is wrong," Mr Carter said, and the three disbelievers smirked at the unfortunate detective with glances of satisfied triumph.

"He did steal something."

The smirks died away, and the astonished faces rounded again on Mr Carter. "He stole all the cups from the library. The police are waiting there now to see Jennings and Darbishire. Get dressed quickly, and go and see them before breakfast."

Mr Carter walked out, leaving a bubbling cauldron of excitement to boil over, as soon as the door shut behind him.

When the two boys reached the library, they found that the Headmaster and Mr Wilkins were in the room. The Head-master introduced them to Sergeant Hutchinson and then left, with a curt instruction that the boys were to report to him after breakfast.

Mr Wilkins said nothing, but sat by the window staring moodily across the rugger pitch.

Sergeant Hutchinson soon put the boys at their ease. They told him what had happened the previous evening, and he made notes from time to time in his little book. Then Jennings said: "And it wasn't only last night, you know. I've seen lights there before, but I was just waiting to get some evidence and stuff before I pounced."

"You needn't worry about the other times," Sergeant Hutchinson smiled. "Mr Carter's told me all about that."

"Mr Carter! D'you mean to say he knew and never did a thing about catching them?" This was astounding. What deep game could his house-master be playing?

"It's all quite simple, really," the sergeant explained; and he told them how last night had been an exception to Hawkins' rule of arriving with clockwork regularity.

"Gosh," Jennings gasped, as light dawned. "So if I'd gone over there any other night, I should have cooked up the most frantic bish you could think of!"

The boys' evidence did not amount to much. They had not seen their assailant so they could give no description of him, but when Jennings told of how he had telephoned the police station, the sergeant looked puzzled.

"You say you actually spoke to the police station on the phone last night?" he queried, for he knew that the first news of the robbery had come from Mr Carter.

"Yes. I spoke to Sergeant somebody or other. He said he didn't want to come to the san in case he caught the measles, instead of the burglar."

A loud "Corwumph" came from the direction of the window, and Mr Wilkins said hurriedly: "That's all right, Sergeant. I can explain all about that, afterwards."

The sergeant looked again at his notebook. "When this man locked you up, did you see whether he was carrying anything?"

"I'm sure he wasn't," Jennings answered, "because he used both hands to drag us across the hall."

"He'd got a torch though," Darbishire added, "but I think he put it in his pocket, and after he'd locked us in we could hear him running away, so he couldn't have had the cups with him then."

138

Sergeant Hutchinson had already reached this conclusion. The most likely explanation was that the burglar's first call had been at the sanatorium. It had yielded nothing, except a surprise visit from Jennings and Darbishire; and having dealt with them, the man must then have made his way over to the main building. He had probably broken into the library at the same time that Mr Carter and the rescue party were releasing the boys from the locked room, and he had made his escape before their return.

One thing was certain. The burglar could not have known very much about the nightly routine of the school, or he would not have paid his illegal visit at a time when Hawkins was normally engaged in sweeping-up operations. The sergeant was inclined to think that the robbery was the work of some tramp chancing his luck – a tramp who had no idea of how slender the thread was on which his luck had held.

"I'd better have a look at this sleeve button," the sergeant said, and Jennings' face fell. He could not imagine Sherlock Holmes having to admit to the police that he had lost a vital clue.

"Well, never mind," the sergeant consoled him, when Jennings explained that it was missing, "perhaps we'll be able to find it later on."

There were tomatoes on fried bread for breakfast, but Jennings was unable to enjoy his favourite dish. He could have kicked himself for losing the only clue which might throw some light on the mystery. He took a far more serious view of his failure than Sergeant Hutchinson did, for Jennings did not realise the difficulties of tracing the unknown burglar, even if the missing button could be found.

Then, there was the interview with the Headmaster, scheduled to take place after breakfast. This, in itself, was enough to make the tomatoes on fried bread turn to dust and ashes; which was a pity, for Mrs Caffey had been specially careful not to let this happen before the food left the kitchen.

The dining-hall pulsed with excited comment. "I bet old General Merridew will be furious," said Venables. "I'd like to hear what he says to the Head." He drew an exciting, but inaccurate picture of an angry general thumping the study desk and waving his walking stick, while M W B Pemberton-Oakes, Esq., stood shuffling uneasily from one foot to the other.

Atkinson was furious to think that a thief could be so heartless. "It's nothing short of hairy cheek," he protested, "pinching our cups on the very day we've simply *got* to have them. Gosh, I'd like to get hold of that burglar!"

"You wouldn't," said Darbishire, with feeling. "I've done it, so I know."

He was not enjoying the meal either. Like Jennings, he voted the Wednesday menu the best breakfast of the week; for their great delight was to eat the tomatoes first, and then spread their marmalade on the fried bread. But today, even this attraction palled before the thought of the visit to the Headmaster's study.

"Never mind, Darbi," Bromwich major comforted him. "If they catch him, there might even be a wizard reward – perhaps, say, a hundred pounds even, and you and Jennings ought to get some of it, by rights."

They argued fiercely about the reward, which ranged from a thousand pounds, at the highest estimate, to six of the best for breaking bounds, at the more pessimistic end of the scale.

"Well, what's going to happen after the sports?" Temple wanted to know. "The old geezer can't dish out a cup, if it's not there."

140

"Perhaps he'll give us an IOU," suggested Martin-Jones. "But it'll be a bit thick, having to beef round the track all the afternoon for a piece of paper, and all the time the burglar's gloating over our cup, and perhaps, even, drinking his tea out of it."

There was plenty to talk about during breakfast, and much of the conversation was about the gallant efforts of the *Lin. Ct. Det. Ag.*; but somehow, Jennings and Darbishire were unable to enjoy the praise that was lavished upon them.

Mr Pemberton-Oakes, when they went to see him, lavished no praise; instead, he spoke of "misdirected energy," "foolhardy stupidity," and "wanton disobedience."

"Normally," he said, "I am not in favour of corporal punishment. I do not consider it to be a good thing" – and though they did not say so, Jennings and Darbishire agreed wholeheartedly with this opinion.

"However," he continued, laying aside his good principles in a way that the boys thought was treacherous, "I think that in this case…ah …um…" He left the sentence unfinished, and turned towards the cupboard, where he kept the cane that he professed to dislike.

They left the study smarting under the injustice of grown-ups, and the corporal punishment of which nobody was in favour. The latter was soon over, but Jennings was upset because the grown-up mind would not see that he had acted from the highest motives. School rules were all very well when life was running smoothly, but surely one must cut through red tape at times of crisis.

Nobody seemed able to concentrate on their work during the lessons before morning break. Wandering minds would wrench themselves away from the burglary, only to veer off out of the window to the running track, or the long-jump pit; for the playing field was dotted with little flags and white-washed lines, marking out running lanes and starting points.

From his desk near the window, Jennings could follow the course of the quarter-mile track, until it disappeared out of sight behind a clump of bushes at the end of the field, and once or twice, he caught sight of Sergeant Hutchinson and a constable moving briskly between the main buildings and the sanatorium.

During break, Darbishire led Jennings down to the tuck-box room.

"That book I was reading about athletics has got some super-spivish hints in it," he said. "It says athletes ought to eat a lot of fruit, so I vote we spend break tucking into my fruit parcel, that my father sent me." He opened his tuck-box and produced an assortment of bulging paper bags.

"It'll take more than that lot to make you win the half-mile," Jennings said, "and anyway, you should have started weeks ago – it's too late now."

"I don't see why," Darbishire argued. "We shall just have to make up for lost time. There's still about four hours before the sports, and if we eat, say, three or four pounds of apples and a box of dates and half a dozen oranges and all these bananas, it ought to make us run like blinko this afternoon."

"Yes, but it won't make us run the right way. We shall be running up to Matron to say we've got collywobbles, and can we go to bed."

As they sat on their tuck-boxes and munched apples, Jennings' mind was still on the burglary. Presently he said: "I wonder if Sherlock Holmes could have solved it?"

"Of course he could," his friend assured him. "He'd just say: 'Elementary, my dear Jennings – you know my methods.' You told me yourself that's how he did it."

"Well, if *he* could solve it, why can't *we*? Here we've been practising nearly all the term with Morse buzzers and telescopes and secret codes and things, and as soon as we get a real problem we don't know where to start." The chief detective glared at his assistant, as though holding him responsible.

"Well, don't look at me like that," Darbishire defended himself. "My nerves haven't quite gone back into shape after last night, and anyway, if anyone's made a bish, you have." He took a large bite of apple and added accusingly: "Who lost the button? I bet Sherlock Holmes wouldn't have done that."

"Perhaps he wouldn't," Jennings reasoned, "but that's because he's only a chap in a book. It's miles easier for them. Now, if we were chaps in a story, we could start off by suspecting the person who's least likely to have done it. The criminal always turns out to be someone you'd never dream of."

"Well, let's do that then," suggested Darbishire. "Go and tell the Head you suspect him of burgling his own school."

Jennings threw his apple-core at his assistant. "Don't be so bats – you know what I mean. In a detective story, the thief would turn out to be someone like – " He broke off and stared into space with unseeing eyes. When he spoke again, his voice had taken on a new note.

"I say, Darbi, you don't think it could have been Old Nightie, do you?"

"What?"

Jennings jumped up and paced the tuck-box room with official strides. "Why not?" he demanded. "In the first place, no one would dream of suspecting him. Besides, he was supposed to be in the san, when he said he wasn't there. Golly, if only we could find out if he's got a coat without a button on it."

"He has," said Darbishire helpfully, "I've seen it."

"Have you? When?"

"Oh, last week sometime. There were no buttons on it at all, and it was done up with safety pins. I saw him coming out of the boiler-room."

Jennings clicked his tongue reproachfully. "Darbishire, you've got as much sense as that apple-core. I don't care if Old Nightie had got fifty million coats without buttons last week. The one I want is a coat that *had* got a button last week, and hasn't got one now."

"Oh, I see," replied Darbishire humbly. "I'm sorry if I'm a bit feeble as a detective, but I did notice one thing which proves Old Nightie couldn't have done it."

"What?"

"Well, when he came over last night with Mr Carter and Old Wilkie, he wasn't wearing his jacket; he was in his shirt sleeves."

Jennings considered this theory and rejected it.

"But, don't you see, that was part of his bluff? He had to take his coat off when he came back with Mr Carter, in case I spotted the button."

"You couldn't have spotted it. It wasn't there to spot. It was in your dressing-gown pocket."

"Oh, don't be such a prehistoric remains. You're muddling things up, and it's quite clear really. Now this is what I think happened. Old Nightie locked us up, so that everyone would think there was a burglar about, and then he beetled off to the libe and pinched the cups. After that, he met Mr Carter and pretended he'd never even been over to the san – we know that happened because Sergeant Hutchinson told us before breakfast – and that gave him an ali – ali – something."

"Alligator?"

"No, alibi, that's it!"

"But what does Sergeant Hutchinson want an alibi for?"

Jennings swung round on his assistant angrily.

"Are you trying to be funny, Darbi? You may be as crazy as two coots, but I should have thought even Binns minor would have understood what I meant."

Darbishire removed his spectacles and polished them with his tie. "I know perfectly well what you meant," he said mildly, "and as a matter of fact, I was trying to be funny."

"But don't you realise how serious it is?"

"It'll be a wizard sight more serious for you, if you go and tell Old Nightie he's a crook – dash it all, Jen, he's been here since before Julius Caesar's time. If he wanted to pinch anything, he'd have done it ages ago."

"I'm not so sure," Jennings argued. "How do we know he hasn't been planning this burglary for years, but it wasn't till last night he had the chance to put the blame on somebody else. Anyway, I'm going to tell Sergeant Hutchinson my theory, when I see him again."

He did not see the sergeant again that morning, for the Headmaster had asked him to postpone his inquiries until late in the afternoon. Mr Pemberton-Oakes disliked having policemen on the premises at all, and considered that to have them trapesing about the grounds while the sports were in progress, would ruin the keen athletic atmosphere that should prevail on these occasions.

Sergeant Hutchinson agreed to return to Dunhambury for the time being, for there was much to be done at the police station. A description of the missing property had been sent out, and inquiries were being made at places where the thief might try to dispose of his plunder. He was not expecting to make an early arrest, and the few matters which he had yet to attend to at the school could be left until the sports were over.

The police car was turning out of the drive as the bell rang to signal the end of break, and Jennings and Darbishire turned reluctant footsteps towards their classroom.

14

The Headmaster is not Amused

"What's the next lesson, somebody?" Martin-Jones demanded, as Form III trooped into their classroom after morning break.

Several somebodies consulted their timetables.

"It's Latin with the Head," groaned Venables. "Oh, gosh, and I made an ozard bish of learning my prep."

"That's all right," Rumbelow consoled him. "There's quite a rare chance he won't be able to take us this lesson. He was talking to that police sergeant five minutes ago, so with any luck, he'll be too busy to come in."

"Don't you believe it; I've been caught that way before," Venables answered, and they all opened their Latin books for a last minute revision of the pronoun, *hic haec hoc*.

"I bet he tests us," said Bromwich major, fumbling to find the page. "I wrote it out last night, but I haven't the vaguest idea how it goes."

"It goes like a machine-gun," Jennings told him. Crouching in his desk, like a tail-gunner in his turret, he aimed his ruler at an imaginary enemy fighter. "*Hic hic hic…haec haec haec… hoc hoc hoc…hic haec hoc…hic haec hoc…hic haec hoc*," the gun spattered raucously.

Form III was delighted with this foolproof method of learning Latin pronouns, and hastened to join up as Roman rear-gunners in Caesar's fighter legion.

"Wizard wheeze!" sang out Temple, hastily making a patent bomb-sight out of a paper-fastener. "Here comes a jet-propelled Feminine Ablative blazing away in Latin, *hac hac hac ...hac hac hac...hac hac hac.*"

"I'm an anti-aircraft Accusative Singular," Bromwich major announced; "*hunc hanc hoc...hunc hanc hoc...hunc hanc hoc.*"

"Take cover," warned Nuttall, "Genitive dive-bomber zooming down to zero feet. Eee-ow-ow! *Horum harum horum ...horum harum horum...* Eee-ow-ow!"

"Ancient Roman wireless operator, sending out Morse signals in Latin," Venables joined in, and jerked out in brisk, staccato fashion, "*Hi hae haec...hos has haec...* Go on, Atkinson, you answer me."

"Okay. *Huic huic huic...huic huic huic...huic huic huic,*" flashed back the transmitter from the Atkinson control tower.

The classroom throbbed with the activity of the Roman Air Force. Caesar's Bomber Squadron, led by Wing-Imperator Rumbelow, set off on a mission to divide all Gaul into three parts with the aid of well-placed blockbusters; but they were intercepted by a strong force of enemy fighters, and had to return to base and take cover beneath their desk-lids.

"*Hac hac hac...hac hac hac...hac hac hac...*" the Feminine Ablatives blazed away from the back row.

"*Hunc hanc hoc...hunc hanc hoc...*" replied the heavy flak of the Accusative Singulars, from just below the master's desk.

"*Horurn harum horum...horum harum horum ...horum harum horum...*" droned the Genitive Plural dive-bombers.

"*Huic huic huic...huic huic huic...*" clicked the wireless operators, tapping their forefingers on rulers held firm by desk-lids.

Never had Form III shown such interest in their pronouns, and the aerial battle was at its height, when the Headmaster walked in.

147

Immediately, engines cut out and machine-guns jammed in mid-burst. But the unfortunate pilot of J for Jennings, who was suffering from combat fatigue, was slow to react to this new danger. His plane had been hit by Nominative Singular tracer bullets in the second row – his engines were stalling, and his machine was about to blow up.

"*Hic-haec-hoc...hic-haec-hoc...hic-haec-hoc...* B-A-N-G!" were the words which greeted the Headmaster as he stood in the doorway. He walked to the master's desk in ominous silence.

"Which boy went on talking, after I came in?" he demanded.

Jennings raised his hand. "I wasn't really what you'd call talking, sir."

The Headmaster raised his eyebrows.

"Then what were you doing?"

"I – I spoke, sir."

"You were not talking, but you spoke. I regret that my simple mind is unable to detect any difference between the two things."

"I was learning my Latin pronouns out loud, sir."

"I see. And since when has the pronoun *Hic* ended with the word Bang?"

"It came out by accident, sir."

"Really!" The Headmaster turned and walked along the rows, inspecting the exercise books in which the boys had written out their preparation. The copies were neat, for Mr Pemberton-Oakes had a horror of slovenly writing, and when he arrived at Jennings' desk, a shadow of annoyance passed over his features.

"You know perfectly well that I never allow pencil to be used in exercise books. Why didn't you use your pen?"

"It broke, sir," Jennings admitted unhappily, and produced the two halves for the Headmaster's inspection. At one time, the wooden penholder had been six inches long, but absent-minded chewing had reduced it to half this length; and the two fragments, which Jennings held out before the Head-master's horrified gaze, consisted of a crossed nib in a metal socket, and an inch of ink-stained wood, splayed out like a shaving-brush.

Mr Pemberton-Oakes averted his eyes from the miserable object.

"It broke!" he murmured softly. "Of its own accord, naturally. I notice, Jennings, you don't say 'I was talking' and 'I broke it,' but '*it* came out by accident' and '*it* broke.' Most unsatisfactory; bring your Latin book up to my desk. I shall test you orally."

Back to his desk strode the Headmaster. He perched himself on the high stool, and glanced at the cover of the book which Jennings laid before him. Again his face darkened.

"Jennings," he said, "when the author wrote this admirable book, he saw fit to call it *A New Latin Grammar*. Had he wished to call it *A New Eating Grammar*, I have no doubt he would have done so."

Jennings shuffled uncomfortably from one foot to the other. He had whiled away many a dull prep in making suitable alterations to his textbook, but he had not reckoned on having his handiwork inspected by the Headmaster.

"Of course, I cannot hold you responsible." There was a note of irony in the Headmaster's voice. "Your pen obviously decided to alter the lettering, before it accidentally broke itself in half."

"No sir; I did it, sir."

"Really! And do you know what happens to boys who scribble in text-books?"

149

"Yes, sir."

The Headmaster opened the book and found that the author's work had been revised in some detail. Pencilled sketches of knights in armour and daffodils in bloom adorned the margin; racing cars swerved between columns of irregular verbs. On the title page was written:

> *"If this book should dare to roam,*
> *Box its ears and send it home."*

This was followed by the owner's address which took up eleven lines, and gave full details of the continent, hemisphere and solar system to which the straying volume should be returned.

"This," said the Headmaster severely, "has ruined a perfectly good book."

"Yes, sir. You did tell us to write our names in them though, sir."

"I am unaware that I instructed you to smear illiterate doggerel all over the covers."

With obvious distaste, he read aloud:

> *"Latin is a language, as dead as dead can be.*
> *It killed the ancient Romans, and now it's killing me."*

He glanced round the room, and the boys in the front row hastily turned the pages of their Latin books to cover up any poetic efforts of their own. His voice was heavy with irony as he turned back to Jennings and said, "What brilliant wit! What biting satire! What a masterly condemnation of the teaching profession!"

"Oh, I don't mean it's *really* killing me, sir," the poet explained. "You have to take the poem meteorologically, sir."

The Headmaster rose with a dignified look. He did not actually call for bell, book and candle, but by the time he had finished, Jennings looked as woebegone as the bedraggled Jackdaw of Rheims.

The first part of the punishment sounded fair enough – Jennings was to pay five shillings for a new copy of the Latin book out of his pocket-money; but as the full meaning of the rest of the punishment became clear, the Drake House members of Form III stifled groans of despair.

"…and you will stay in this afternoon during the sports and write out your preparation twelve times with an unbroken pen. I am aware that your house is relying on you to compete in various races, and this will, perhaps, bring it home to all, that boys who spoil expensive text-books punish not only themselves, but their friends and colleagues as well."

Jennings went white with misery as he heard his sentence passed, and his eyes were moist as he returned to his desk in the hushed classroom. He felt that the bottom had dropped out of his world. If he could not compete in the sports, those few vital points would be lost, and Drake would have no chance of winning the contest. He would willingly have written out his preparation fifty times and paid for a dozen books, if only the punishment could be postponed until later in the day. What would his house say? What would Mr Carter think? To let the house down at a moment like this was the most serious crime that anyone could imagine.

Mr Pemberton-Oakes knew that the boy was feeling the punishment keenly, but this was the second time in one morning that Jennings had crossed his path, and he was determined to stand no more nonsense.

"And now," he said, "we will have a test on *hic haec hoc*."

Jennings came out with top marks in the test. He tried as he had never tried before, hoping that the Headmaster might relent; but the hope was vain.

Five minutes before the lesson ended, there was a knock at the door and Mary, one of the housemaids, came in.

"Excuse me, sir," she whispered in the Headmaster's ear. "There's a gentleman called to see Mr Jennings."

The Headmaster looked surprised. "*Mister* Jennings?" he repeated.

"That's what he said, sir, but I expect he meant Master Jennings, really. The gentleman says his name's Mr Russell, sir. I've shown him into the library."

"Mr Russell?" The name meant nothing to the Headmaster and he inquired: "Do you know a Mr Russell, Jennings? Is he a relation?"

"No, sir," Jennings replied blankly.

"H'm. A friend of the family, perhaps, who has come down to watch the sports?"

"I don't know, sir – he might be."

The Headmaster turned to the waiting housemaid. "Tell Mr Russell that I will send Jennings to see him at the end of the lesson, and say that I shall be pleased to make his acquaintance as soon as I am free."

"Yes, sir."

Mary returned to the library, where Mr Russell was wondering what type of man his prospective customer would turn out to be. So far the salesman was delighted, for his first impressions were that Mr Jennings was a man of such obvious wealth that he would not quibble over the price of an expensive ciné camera.

Mr Russell had arrived at Dunhambury by train, and had hired a taxi for the last part of the journey. Everything had confirmed his employer's theory that Linbury Court was the home of the squire of the manor. The taxi had turned in through ornate, wrought-iron gates, and had sped up a long drive, lined with thick yew hedges, which had prevented him from seeing the rugger pitches behind them.

When the taxi came to rest before the wide sweep of steps leading to the front door, Mr Russell was sure that he had arrived at one of the stately homes of England. He was not far out in his judgment, for the house had originally been the country seat of the fourth Lord Linbury, and from the outside, it bore little trace of the changes which had taken place within its walls.

He was led across a large entrance hall and shown into a well-stocked library. Mr Russell did not read the titles of the books, or he might have been surprised at the squire's strong liking for boys' stories. But he noted with approval the shields painted with public school crests; these, obviously, were the coats-of-arms of different branches of the extensive Jennings family.

When Mary returned and asked him if he would wait a few minutes, he was confident that the ciné camera was as good as sold already.

"Certainly," he smiled. "What a charming room this is. I think Linbury Court is one of the finest country houses I've ever visited."

"Yes, sir," said Mary and prepared to go, but the salesman was anxious to learn all he could of the squire's interests.

"I imagine it needs a large staff to look after a place this size," he said casually.

"Oh, yes, it does," the housemaid agreed. "There's me and three other maids and cook and Mrs Caffey and two house-parlour men and Robinson for the odd jobs. Then there's the outdoor staff as well."

Mr Russell smiled. If the squire employed so many servants, he must be a man who enjoyed spending money. "I take it that Mr Jennings is a gentleman of some fortune?"

Mary stared at him for a moment, and then broke into an idiotic giggle. "*Mister* Jennings!" she tittered. "Hee! hee! hee!"

Wondering whether the girl was half-witted, Mr Russell turned to the squire's interests in sport. He had borrowed a book about country life the previous day, and had spent the train journey to Dunhambury in learning all he could about the habits of rural gentlemen. No one could say that Mr Russell was not thorough.

"I suppose there's plenty of hunting, shooting and fishing and all that sort of thing?"

Mary giggled again. "There's no hunting, sir. There's riding, though."

"Oh, yes, of course. And shooting?"

"Yes, sir," Mary replied, remembering Mr Topliss' weekly class in the tiny shooting-range behind the gymnasium. She would have been surprised if she had known that her answer stirred Mr Russell's mind to visions of nobility and gentry, in hairy tweeds, sitting on shooting sticks, while keepers beat the surrounding foliage for pheasants.

Perhaps he's a military type, Mr Russell thought, and aloud he asked: "Has Mr Jennings any special rank or title?"

Waves of helpless giggles engulfed the housemaid. Either this chap with the camera was a lunatic, or he was trying to be funny. Fancy asking such questions about a ten-year-old boy in Form III!

"What I meant was," Mr Russell explained, "is he a Colonel, for instance, or a Brigadier, or – "

"Hee! hee! hee! hee!" Mary tried hard to control herself, but even the thought of what Mrs Caffey would say failed to stem the tittering flow of giggles. "No, he's not in the army," she managed to say – "at least, not yet, he isn't."

She felt the giggles coming on again, and turned and bolted for the door with a breathless: "Excuse me."

"Here, don't go," called Mr Russell. "Wait – " The door shut behind the helpless housemaid, and Mr Russell was left wondering what on earth was the matter with the girl.

He unslung the Grossman Ciné Camera de Luxe from his shoulder and placed it on the table with the small suitcase, in which he carried a further supply of coloured film. Then he settled himself in an armchair.

15

The Friend of the Family

Mr Russell had not long to wait. After a few moments the door opened, and he sprang to his feet to greet his wealthy client.

"Good mor – Oh!"

A boy in a grey suit, with brown hair and a wide-awake look in his eyes, came into the room.

"Please, sir," said the boy, "I'm Jennings."

"You're – ? You mean, you're Mr Jennings' son?"

This struck Jennings as being rather a silly question. "Yes, of course I am. I'd have to be, wouldn't I?"

"Yes, yes, of course. What I meant was, it's your father whom I've come to see."

Jennings looked at his visitor curiously. "Oh, but my father doesn't live here; he lives at Haywards Heath. He just comes down to see me for the weekend sometimes."

"But surely, this is his address isn't it?"

"Gosh, no," said Jennings. "You wouldn't expect to find him still at school at his age, would you?"

The room swam before Mr Russell's eyes. "What?" he gasped, as a ghastly suspicion flooded his mind. "Did you say *at school*? Do you – do you mean to tell me this is a school?"

156

"Yes, of course," Jennings answered, wondering why this strange man was behaving in such an odd manner. "Linbury Court Preparatory School."

"Good heavens!" the salesman murmured weakly. The ghastly suspicion had changed to a beacon which was shedding light on the explanation of the whole business. "Well of all the – Then you must be J C T Jennings!"

"Yes," said Jennings. He thought that had been clear from the start.

"And it was you who wrote to us about the ciné camera?"

Suddenly Jennings, too, was conscious of a light dawning. "Oh, golly!" he said aghast. "Is *that* who you are?"

"It certainly is," retorted Mr Russell angrily. "And I've come all this way to sell you one."

Jennings was horrified.

"But I never meant you to *come*," he explained. "I never even asked you to. I only wanted a catalogue. The advertisement said I could have one, if I wanted one."

"You didn't tell me you were a schoolboy," Mr Russell argued, leaning heavily against the table. "You said you wanted to buy a camera, and here I've come down from London – "

"Well, I still want to," Jennings assured him, "only I'm a bit short of dosh – er – money."

Mr Russell seized the camera in its leather case, and waved it under Jennings' nose. "Do you know how much this camera costs?" he asked fiercely. "Ninety-five guineas!... Ninety-five guineas! And how much have you got?"

"Three and sevenpence," mumbled Jennings apologetically.

"Three and sevenpence. Cor!!!"

Mr Russell paced up and down the library, swinging the camera savagely by its strap. When his feelings were again under control, he turned to the unhappy object before him and said: "Listen, my boy. You've got me here under false pretences. Smart notepaper, imposing address, embossed crest and all that carry-on. What were we to think?"

"I'm sorry," said Jennings.

"Sorry! So I should think. I've given up a whole day, cancelled important engagements, travelled sixty miles to get here, and all for what?" he demanded, waving his arms dramatically. "To be offered three and sevenpence for a ninety-five guinea movie camera!"

"But, Mr Russell, I never meant – "

"For the first time in my life, I've been taken for a mug. Its absurd – it's ridiculous." Stooping until his face was on a level with Jennings' distressed features, he barked: "When I get back to London and tell the manager I've been wasting time and money like this, he'll – he'll foam at the mouth and explode!"

Jennings' eyes became round as saucers at this entrancing prospect. But Mr Russell retired to an armchair, and thought hard.

First, he thought how furious he was, and how he would like to give J C T Jennings a good hiding. And then he thought of Mr Catchpole foaming at the mouth and exploding, and the idea was so ludicrous that, in spite of his anger, he stopped scowling, and a slow grin spread over his face. He was a kind-hearted man, and there was something about the wide-awake look in the eyes of the boy standing before him that made it impossible for Mr Russell to go on being angry for long. Besides, he reflected, the joke was on Mr Catchpole – for it was he who had been so sure that J C T Jennings was a wealthy aristocrat.

Mr Russell had a keen sense of humour, and now that his first outburst of wrath was over, he began to see the funny side of things. Ten seconds later, he started to laugh.

Jennings gaped in surprise at the rapid change in the salesman's manner. Only a minute before, he had been pacing the room in towering anger, and now he was sitting in the armchair, shaking with silent mirth.

Mr Russell had a peculiar laugh which sounded like a railway engine: he never let himself go wholeheartedly, but seemed, instead, to bottle it all up inside him, and only a curious *choof-chooof* sound was allowed to escape through the safety-valve of his lips.

"I can just imagine what the manager will say when I tell him," Mr Russell said, when his railway engine had *choof-choofed* to a stop. " 'Your Mr Jennings,' I'll tell him – and I can just picture his face when I say it – 'Your Mr Jennings is a… *Choof-choof-choof-choof!'* "

He started to shake again as he recalled Mr Catchpole's words; " 'Wealthy aristocrat,' I'll tell him… 'Squire of the village… Everybody who is anybody in his part of Sussex will be wanting a…' *Choof-choof-choof-choof!*… 'Careful how I handle important customers!' Oh dear, oh dear!"

He *choofed* quietly, but the tears trickling down his face showed how rich Mr Russell considered the joke to be. "Three and sevenpence for our most expensive… *Choof! choof! choof!* No wonder the maid thought I was up the pole. Hunting, shooting and fishing! She must have thought I was… *Choof-choof-choof!* Well, thank goodness I can see the funny side of it."

He pulled himself together, and dabbed his eyes with his handkerchief, while Jennings stared at him with a mixture of amazement and despair.

"I wish I could see the funny side of it," he said.

"Well, can't you?"

"No. It hasn't got a funny side for me."

"Nonsense," said Mr Russell gaily. "If I can take it as a joke, with all the business I'm losing, I'm sure you can."

"But you don't understand. The Headmaster's coming along in a minute, to find out why you've come to see me."

"Is he, by Jove! He'll laugh himself silly when I tell him what's happened."

"No, he won't." Jennings shook his head sadly. "You don't know Headmasters. They're not good at seeing things like other people, and there's a frantic hoo-hah going on already."

"There's a *what*?"

It was not often that Jennings confided his troubles to a complete stranger, but he did so now, because Mr Russell seemed anxious to listen. He explained that twice already that morning he had fallen foul of the Headmaster, and was being kept in, when he should be helping his house in the sports.

"...and it's all because I put my name and address and a sort of poem thing in my Latin book, and everyone turns *Latin* into *Eating*, anyway."

"Come again?" queried the perplexed salesman.

"Oh, you wouldn't understand," Jennings told him, "but it's super-ozard squared, because Drake will all be as sick as mud, and Mr Carter won't say anything at all; and that'll be worse, because I like him, and if you let him down it's awful. And I got full marks in the test, hoping he'd let me off for Drake's sake, but he never did."

There was much that Mr Russell did not understand, but he gathered enough to realise that the future outlook was cloudy.

"And it'll be worse in a minute," Jennings continued, "because the Head will say I shouldn't have written to you, and he'll think I asked you to come down on purpose, and we're not allowed to have anyone to see us, except relations and friends, and there'll be another row about that."

Mr Russell listened with a grave expression. He could not explain why, but his sympathy was aroused by this boy who had caused him so much trouble. The situation seemed serious, and Mr Russell rose to the occasion like a hero.

"Well, that's all right," he said cheerfully. "If friends are allowed to visit you, there's nothing to worry about I'm a friend of yours, now. We've known each other for nearly ten minutes."

"I'm not sure that you'd count," Jennings said, doubtfully. "You don't even know my family."

Mr Russell thought for a moment; then he said, quite truthfully, "Well, as a matter of fact, I do happen to know a Mr Jennings. He lives at er – um – "

"Haywards Heath?"

"I'm just trying to remember. It might have been."

"Of course, if you really know my father that would make all the difference. Gosh, wouldn't it be wizard if you did!"

The salesman frowned thoughtfully at the toe of his shoe. The only Mr Jennings that he could recall was a vague business acquaintance whom he had not seen for years. He hardly remembered what he looked like, or whether he was young or old, tall or short. On the other hand, who could say whether it might not be the same man?

"Well," he said slowly, "it's just as likely to be him as any other Mr Jennings, isn't it?"

Jennings had no time to reply, for at that moment the Headmaster arrived to inspect the visitor for himself.

"Good morning, Mr – er – um – "

"Russell."

"Ah, yes – Mr Russell."

The salesman felt the Headmaster's eye examining him, from his glossy black hair to his glossy black shoes; for Mr Pemberton-Oakes was careful to protect the boys in his charge from unsuitable visitors. Then Jennings was sent to wait outside in the hall, and as soon as the door was shut the

Headmaster said: "May I inquire, Mr Russell, whether you are a relative of the Jennings' family?"

"No, no. I can't claim to be more than a casual friend – if that; but I used to do business with a Mr Jennings of – of – "

"Haywards Heath?"

"That name does ring a bell certainly. However," he went on hastily, "as I was in the district I decided to call."

"Very kind of you. The boys are always pleased to welcome friends of the family."

The Headmaster thawed considerably, and Mr Russell knew that he had passed his test as a suitable Sports Day visitor.

His first impulse was to chat politely for a few minutes, and then excuse himself on the grounds of urgent business, and make his way back to London. He had done all that could be expected of him, and had helped his young friend to avoid further trouble in the matter of unwelcome visitors; but as Mr Russell sat listening to the Headmaster's lengthy opinion of the weather, he suddenly thought that, as a friend of the family, he should do more. A good friend, for example, might bring up the question of Jennings' detention during the sports.

He was far too good a salesman, however, to make such a request outright. Instead he remarked: "I was hoping I might be allowed to watch the sports this afternoon. I'm sure Mr Jennings would be interested to hear a first hand account of the 440 when I see him again – which may not be for a long time," he added to himself.

"I am afraid that Jennings will not be competing," the Headmaster replied. "A little matter of discipline, you understand."

Mr Russell rose to his feet and casually picked up the ciné camera from the table. "That's a pity; you see, I've brought my camera. I was just thinking what excellent material the sports would make, for a colour film. Have you got a projector you could show it with?"

"Oh, yes, we have films every Wednesday evening. I hire them from a film library in London."

"But how much more satisfactory to show a film which you have actually made yourself," said Mr Russell persuasively. This was the moment for a sales talk, and he made the most of it.

"I see it something like this... Imagine a Wednesday evening – the school sitting tense with excitement, waiting for the film to start. The lights go down – a caption appears on the screen – The Annual Sports. Then, a long shot of the grounds with the school in the distance, the coloured flags fluttering gaily in the breeze, the sun streaming down and the boys streaming out, in bright Technicolor blazers. Next, a medium shot of the runners lining up for the start... Close-up of the starter's finger trembling on the trigger of the gun... They're off!"

Mr Russell's voice thrilled with excitement, as he pressed on with his running commentary. "Then we switch to a crowd scene... Excited spectators shouting themselves hoarse... The camera pans back to the runners... Number 3 trips up, and Number 5 crashes down on top of him... Number 4's in the lead, in the greatest race of the day... Close-up of his determined expression!"

The commentator set his jaw and clenched his teeth in an all-out effort, and noted that Mr Pemberton-Oakes was sitting forward on the edge of his chair, drinking in every detail of the scene.

"The camera tracks to the finishing tape," Mr Russell hissed breathlessly, through still clenched teeth. "We see a medium shot of the judges trying to look calm beneath their mounting excitement – and what excitement! Oh dear, oh dear, there's never been anything like it!"

The salesman was now pacing the room and scattering handfuls of tense atmosphere in the direction of the fireplace. "Close-up of the stopwatch ticking remorselessly on… Tick…tick…tick!"

The Headmaster stared; he seldom met human beings who carried on in this unusual way.

"Back to the running track… We see a long shot of the runners… They're in the straight… Number 4 is in the lead… Number 1 is coming up on the inside… He's gaining… he's …he's done it!… Number 1 wins! The camera shoots the smiling winner being slapped on the back by admiring friends… Next a close-up of the winner shaking hands with the Headmaster. Hold it!… The Headmaster turns full face to the camera, the sunlight picking out the colours of his old school tie. He smiles warmly… Slowly, the picture fades."

Mr Russell sank into an armchair and mopped his brow. "What an idea for a picture!" he murmured ecstatically. "It's an inspiration… It's a masterpiece!"

Mr Pemberton-Oakes would probably have dismissed the sales talk as an undignified exhibition, but for the fact that the subject was dear to his heart. He had for some time been wanting to buy a ciné camera for just such an occasion as this.

"You're right, Mr Russell, you're quite right," he said, rising to his feet with enthusiasm. "A film like that would be a permanent record to thrill future generations, and recapture the memories of old boys visiting their *alma mater* forty years on, when afar and asunder, parted are those who are – "

"Quite. What a pity it's just an idle dream!"

"Idle dream!" The Headmaster was astounded. "But, Mr Russell, you yourself suggested – that is, if you've brought your camera specially, this is just the opportunity."

"On second thoughts, I'd better be getting back to town." He replaced his handkerchief, got up from his chair and began collecting his camera, his suitcase, his overcoat and his gloves.

"Oh, but, surely – " Mr Pemberton-Oakes could not understand it. Had he offended his visitor in some way?

"Well, it's like this, Headmaster. The reason I came down with my camera was to see our friend Jennings. I had hoped to interest him in – " He broke off and smiled: "But that's another story. However, if he's being kept in this afternoon, he won't be able to appear in the film."

The Headmaster assured him that the other seventy-eight boys of Linbury Court would provide excellent material for the camera.

"I'd rather not, if you don't mind," said Mr Russell. "If Jennings could be in it, it would be different, but I think the family would be disappointed if he wasn't in the picture. He usually is, I should imagine. Well, I'm glad to have met you. D'you mind if I telephone for a taxi to take me to the station?"

Mr Pemberton-Oakes thought hard. He would dearly have liked a film of the sports, and it was just the thing that was needed to console the boys for the loss of their cup.

"Now, just a moment, Mr Russell," he said. "Perhaps I was rather hasty, but defacing Latin text-books is a serious matter. Excuse me a moment, will you?"

He opened the library door, and called to Jennings who was sitting forlornly on the staircase, on the opposite side of the hall. Jennings came in expecting more trouble, and could hardly believe his ears when the Headmaster solemnly announced: "I have decided, Jennings, that Drake House will be placed at a disadvantage if they are deprived of one of their entrants for this afternoon's contest. Partly for the sake of your house, therefore, but chiefly because Mr Russell wishes to include the entire school in a cinematic record, I have decided to allow you to compete in the sports."

"Oh, thank you, sir! Thank you ever so much, sir!"

"You will, of course, do your imposition this evening."

"Yes, sir! Willingly, sir! Thank you, sir!"

"I think, perhaps, Mr Russell deserves your thanks more than I do," said the Headmaster ruefully, and Jennings turned to his benefactor almost tearful with gratitude. Mr Russell waved the thanks aside. Making people change their minds was all part of the day's work for an expert salesman.

"Now, Mr Russell," smiled the Headmaster. "May we discuss the film which you are so kindly going to make for us? As a title I would suggest 'Sports Day at Linbury' and underneath that, some apt quotation from the classics such as – er – *Hic...* *Hic...* How does it go? It's on the tip of my tongue. *Hic...*"

Mr Russell could only think of hickory dickory dock, and Jennings' suggestion of *hic haec hoc* was rejected with a frown of annoyance.

"Ah, I have it. *Hic dies, vere mihi festus, atras eximet curas.*"

"Come again?" said Mr Russell, out of his depth.

"*This day, in truth a holiday to me, shall banish idle cares,*" the Headmaster translated. "*Horace, Book 3 – Ode Number 14.*"

"Ah, yes, of course. Good old Horace," nodded Mr Russell, trying to look as though the quotation were familiar to him. Suddenly, he found himself wondering what Mr Catchpole would say, when he discovered that a considerable length of expensive colour film had been used, with no thought of who was going to pay for it. He decided that he could best pacify his manager by giving the firm a free advertisement.

"Now, after this – *Hic* – er – what you said," the salesman went on, "we should have a credit title saying, '*This film appears by kind permission of the Grossman Ciné Camera Co, Ltd.*'"

"Quite," the Headmaster agreed.

"And there's one more we ought to have, too, Mr Russell," Jennings suggested.

"And what is that?"

"*Jennings appears by kind permission of the Headmaster.*"

Mr Russell's shoulders began to shake once more. "*Choof-choof-choof-choof,*" he rippled helplessly.

16

Darbishire Runs a Race

Mr Russell had lunch in the tuck-shop, where a light meal was served to any parents or friends who arrived early.

General Merridew, as the guest of honour, had been invited to sit at the high table in the school dining-hall, but at the last moment, he telephoned to say that he had been delayed, and would not be able to arrive until four-thirty.

"Sorry, Headmaster," his voice crackled over the telephone. "I'm afraid I shall miss most of the sports. Still, I shall be there in time to award the cup, and that's the main thing, eh!"

Award the cup! Mr Pemberton-Oakes had been hoping to break the news gently, when Mrs Caffey's excellent cooking had put the General in a good humour. It was difficult to explain such an unfortunate incident over the telephone. General Merridew was a man of moods, and most people made sure that his mood was a good one, if their news was bad. The Headmaster sighed.

"I regret to say that we have been the victims of a most distressing occurrence," he began into the telephone.

"Speak up; can't hear you. The line's bad. What did you say about pressing currants?"

"You misheard me – I said a distressing occurrence... We had a robbery late last night."

"You had to corroborate *what*, last night?"

"No, no. What I said was…"

"Well, never mind," the line crackled. "Tell me when I get there."

Mr Pemberton-Oakes sat down to luncheon envying the youngest boy in the school. His eye rested upon Binns minor. How delightful life must be for him! No cares, no responsibilities, no hasty-tempered generals to be pacified!

Bins minor stopped talking with his mouth full, when he saw the Headmaster looking at him. How wizard to be an arch-beak, he thought – no maths, no detentions, no one to tick you off when you put your elbows on the table!

The weather had made good its early promise, and the afternoon was as bright and warm as one could hope for in the last week of March. After lunch, Jennings showed Mr Russell round the school, and introduced him to Darbishire, who goggled with embarrassment when he first heard who the visitor was.

Quite soon, however, they were talking like old friends. They told him about the burglary and he *tut-tutted* in sympathy; they told him about the Linbury Court Detective Agency and their hopes of obtaining a camera; they showed him the broken telescope, the mute mouth-organ and the silent Morse buzzer, and the salesman agreed that any detective, famous or otherwise, was worthy of better equipment.

Then the boys went to change, and soon the playing field was speckled with magenta-and-white blazers. They clustered round Mr Carter, like flies round a honey-pot, anxious to be picked for some duty.

"Sir, please, sir, can I do the tinkles on the blower for you, sir?"

"Can you do *what*, Venables?"

"Can I ring the handbell for you, sir, before you start the races?"

"All right, Venables. I hereby appoint you Official Director of Campanology."

"What's that, sir? Something to do with putting up the tea tent?"

"No. Campanology is the science of bell-ringing," Mr Carter told him, for the boys always insisted on having high-sounding titles for their appointments.

"And what can I do, sir?"

Mr Carter considered: "You, Binns minor, can be Chief Salvage Officer and Deputy Armourer."

"Coo, thank you, sir," came the delighted reply. "Thanks most awfully – er – what does all that mean, sir?"

"It means that when I fire the starting pistol, you gather up the used cartridge cases."

"I see, sir. Oh, wizzo! I've always wanted to be a picker-upper. Are you going to use the pistol to start all the races, sir?"

"Of course. What would you expect me to use – a bow and arrow?"

Binns minor thought for a moment and then shrilled delightedly: "Oh, but you don't use a gun for the high-jump, sir. I caught you there, didn't I, sir?"

"You'll be for the 'high-jump,' if you go on asking silly questions," the master smiled, and Binns minor rushed off, to boast to his Form I friends of how he had soundly beaten Mr Carter in a battle of wits.

At two-thirty the bell rang; the starting pistol shattered the tense silence, and the 100 yards, under twelve, was under way.

Drake gathered half the points for this event, but Raleigh jumped into the lead by winning the "Open", for the senior race carried more marks. The Junior 220 was a victory for Raleigh, as their team sprinted round the track to finish first, second and fourth. Jennings was third, and so managed to score one point for his house. Next came the high-jump, and Drake clapped and cheered as their score crept up, and drew level with their rival's.

Mr Russell was enjoying himself. It was a novelty for him to spend an afternoon surrounded by an eager, milling throng of boys, and he dashed about shooting dozens of feet of colour film, heedless of what Mr Catchpole would say when he found out; there were so many exciting shots to be made that the salesman had almost forgotten that the real object of his visit had been to sell the camera. The Headmaster was at his elbow most of the time, dragging him from starting-point to finishing-tape and back, so that nothing should be missed by the camera's recording eye. He, too, was enjoying the afternoon, and had banished all thoughts of burglaries and irate generals to the back of his mind.

"Excellent, Mr Russell," he beamed. "Your shots of the high-jump will be an inspiration for years to come. I shall tell Jennings to write to his father and say how pleased we all were that you were able to come down, today – or perhaps you will be seeing Mr Jennings yourself. I suppose you meet him quite often in the course of business?"

"Well, er – as a matter of fact – oh look, they're lining up for the long-jump," Mr Russell said hastily. "I must get a shot of this. Excuse me," and he dashed across to the long-jump pit, before he could be asked any more awkward questions.

The Headmaster followed at a more dignified pace. "Ah, Wilkins, this is going to be a Sports Day I shall long remember," he said pleasantly, little knowing how true this prophecy was to be. "I'm learning quite a lot about film photography, too. Did you notice how one should crouch low on the ground to take pictures of the high-jumpers? That's either called tracking – or is it panning? or – well, anyway, it's most interesting."

Together, they walked towards the long-jump pit. Mr Wilkins, because of his powerful voice, always announced the results of each event; and although he had a megaphone for this purpose, he seldom needed to use it.

The Official Announcer's Assistant was Bromwich major, who trotted along behind Mr Wilkins, wearing the megaphone on his head like a witch's hat. Whenever he passed a visitor, he raised it politely by the handle.

The long-jump was in full swing when they arrived; Mr Russell was crouching at one end of the pit, so that the oncoming jumpers seemed to be leaping right into the eye of the camera.

Jennings was jumping badly. At his first jump, his foot had passed the take-off board at the end of his run, and Mr Hind, who was judging, had signalled "No jump." Things were no better in the second round; Jennings was so determined not to overstep the mark, that he jumped from a foot behind it, and landed far in the rear of the other competitors.

Now he had one more jump to make. He started his run, reached top speed, arrived at the take-off board with the right foot foremost, and hurled himself high and far – his arms beating the air like wings and his face twisted with effort.

It was the best jump he had ever made; he passed the marks of his rivals by a foot, and in the split second before he landed, he had a glimpse of the crouching Mr Russell, desperately trying to back away out of range.

The photographer was too late, and Jennings landed heavily on top of him knocking him flat on his back. The camera whirred on, automatically recording a distorted close-up of Jennings' left foot, a patch of sky, tree tops and jumbled faces, as it shot round in a wide arc and finished up on the grass, whirring away at Binns minor's ankle socks.

It was lucky that neither Jennings nor Mr Russell was hurt, for the spectators were far more concerned about the fate of the camera. Human beings soon recover from a few bruises, but expensive cameras are more sensitive. They stared spellbound, while Mr Russell examined it, and cheered with relief when he smilingly told them that no damage had been done.

"Gosh, what a hairy bit of luck," gasped Temple. "The faces Jennings made when he was jumping were enough to bust it, and then he has to go and knock it for six with his great feet."

Mr Wilkins broadcast the result, in a voice which was clearly audible above the drone of a passing aeroplane. "First, Jennings...second, Martin-Jones ...third, Johnson."

Drake was now leading by one point. Jennings looked for Darbishire so that they could rejoice together, but his friend had wandered off by himself during the long-jump, and was nowhere to be found.

"Have you seen Darbi anywhere, Bromo?"

"Can't hear a thing," complained Bromwich major. "I was standing next to Old Wilkie, using the megaphone as an ear-trumpet, when he gave out the long-jump result. It went in one ear, and it hasn't come out of the other yet." He wandered off, wondering how long his deafness would last.

Venables rang the bell, and Mr Carter announced: "Throwing the Cricket Ball – Open," and the crowd moved away to another part of the field.

"Ah, there you are, Mr Russell. Not hurt, I hope," the Headmaster inquired.

"Do you mean me, or the camera?"

"I mean both, naturally," replied the Headmaster. "In fact, I was just thinking how very fortunate you are to own a camera like that. I wish I had one."

Mr Russell felt that business was looking up. "This is getting interesting," he murmured to himself.

"It would be invaluable," continued the Headmaster, stepping back quickly to avoid a cricket ball that had veered badly off its course. "Think of the films we could take! Cricket, football, boxing, swimming, concerts, picnics, Scouts – yes, Mr Russell, I'd give a lot to own a ciné camera like yours."

"Ninety-five guineas?"

"I beg your pardon?"

"I'll sell you this one, for that."

The Headmaster blinked in surprise. "Oh, but that's yours – you need it yourself. I wouldn't dream of depriving you. After all, it is your hobby."

Hobby! "If he thinks I trundle around with this gadget six days a week, just for the fun of the thing, he's mistaken," the salesman said to himself. Aloud he said: "Oh, that's all right – I can easily get another one, besides" – he might as well admit it – "selling movie cameras happens to be my business."

"Really! I'd no idea. What a happy coincidence that you should decide to visit Jennings today!"

"Er – yes, quite a coincidence. It must have been fate."

The sale was arranged, and soon Mr Russell was following the Headmaster round the sports field, giving him a lesson in the correct way of using the Grossman Ciné Camera de Luxe.

Raleigh won "Throwing the Cricket Ball." This was unexpected, for Parslow of Drake had a strong arm and was the obvious favourite; but luck was against him, for the ball curved away on its flight, and crashed through the pavilion window.

Darbishire was in the pavilion, getting ready for the half-mile, and he was so startled by the shattering glass, that he shot out of the building at a speed that would not have disgraced a hundred-yards sprinter.

The half-mile was the next event. As it was the longest race, it was usually held last, but the order had been changed because two of the long-jumpers had entered for the 440 and Mr Carter had decided to give them a longer rest between their events. The half-mile, the 440 and the relay were the only events now remaining for which house points could be scored; the rest of the programme consisted of odd items such as the egg-and-spoon and the obstacle races, which were not strictly athletic, and did not count towards winning the competition.

Outside the pavilion, Darbishire ran into Jennings, who took one look at him and said:

"Gosh, Darbi, whatever's the matter? Have you got pneumonia?"

The half-miler was wearing his raincoat on top of his overcoat, and his travelling rug was draped round him from shoulder to ankles.

"No, I haven't got pneumonia, but I'll probably get heat stroke any minute now. I've got two sweaters and my blazer on, under this."

"Whatever for?"

"It says you should, in that book on athletics I was reading. I copied a few notes down – I've got them somewhere."

The athlete's head disappeared beneath the travelling rug; he dug through the various layers of clothing until he reached his blazer pocket. Then his face emerged, warm but smiling, and he waved an envelope through a gap in the rug.

"It says here," he read out, "*The muscles are stimulated to greater degrees of activity by the maintenance of an optimum body heat* – so I'm maintaining the optimum."

"What's that mean?"

"It means it's spivish hot inside all this clutter. I shall take it off when the race starts, of course. I've eaten a lot more fruit, too," he went on. "Five apples and four bananas since lunch, but somehow, I think the book's wrong about that – it hasn't made me feel I could run much faster."

"Half-mile – Open," Mr Carter's voice drifted across to them. "Nuttall, Temple, Clarke, MacTaggart, Binns major and Darbishire."

"Oh golly! This is it! Wish me luck, Jen – it's my big moment."

The two boys scampered across to the starting point, Darbishire's rug trailing from his shoulders, and tripping him up every few yards.

"You look like a Red Indian Chief," Jennings told him.

"Never mind what I look like. If it helps me to maintain the optimist, it may do the trick. My father says that – "

"Darbishire!" shouted the other half-milers, impatient to be away.

"All right, I'm coming." His voice was edgy with nervous excitement as he joined the little group gathered round the starter. There was a short interval while Darbishire shed the load of his garments, and Mr Carter gave them a word of advice.

"You've got to go round the track twice, and it's quite a long way, so don't go too fast to start with. Remember to keep this side of the flags, especially when you're out of sight behind the bushes at the end of the field… On your marks… Get set…"

The crack of the pistol made Darbishire leap like a startled deer, but he soon recovered and settled down to a steady jog trot.

"Go it, Bod," called Venables, as Temple ran by. "Gosh, I hope he wins. Who do you stick up for, Jennings?"

"Darbishire, of course, but he hasn't got an earthly. He runs like a lobster in elastic-sided boots. He's supersonic at the egg-and-spoon though," he finished loyally.

"We'd better be getting ready," Venables suggested. "It's the 440 yards next."

"Oh, there's bags of time yet – they've only just started."

MacTaggart, known as MacBonk, was in the lead, as the six runners rounded the first bend. Halfway round the course, the white line disappeared behind a small clump of bushes, and for a few seconds the runners were not visible. When they appeared again, Temple was leading and MacTaggart had dropped to second place. Darbishire, remembering Mr Carter's advice, had not yet reached the bushes, and was plodding along sixty yards in the rear of the leaders.

"Come on, MacBonk… Good old Bonko!" yelled the Drake supporters, as the runners came down the straight on their first lap.

"Run up, Bod!" shouted the House of Raleigh, as Temple strove to increase his lead.

Jennings would have shouted, "Come on, Darbishire," but unfortunately, his friend was so far behind that he was out of earshot.

"Last lap," called Mr Carter, as Temple and MacTaggart passed him, closely followed by Binns major, Nuttall and Clarke.

"Gosh, it's going to be close," exclaimed Venables, as the runners started on their second lap. "There's not more than ten yards between the lot of them."

"Except for Darbishire," corrected Jennings. "He's still about twenty miles behind."

Darbishire plodded on, doggedly refusing to give up hope. He was disappointed that the trouble he had taken in keeping warm and eating fruit was not *stimulating his muscles to greater degrees of activity* as the book had promised; but there was still a chance that something sensational might happen – a sudden thunderstorm, for instance; perhaps the group of runners two hundred yards ahead would get struck by lightning or attacked by cramp.

He had just completed the first circuit, when his rivals disappeared behind the bushes for the second time, and a moment later Binns major, running strongly, came into view, with Temple and MacTaggart straining to overtake this new rival for first place.

"Now's the time for my extra special burst of speed," Darbishire muttered, and quickened his pace by a good two miles an hour. But the strain began to tell. "Oh, gosh, I wish I hadn't had all those apples," he groaned, as he felt a painful stitch in his side. He struggled on, but the stitch became worse; he would have to take a short rest, or he would never finish the course. He panted to a halt behind the clump of bushes and doubled himself up, touching his toes and drawing in great lungfuls of air. Vaguely, he was aware of the excited tumult in the distance.

"Come on, Bod… Good old Temple!"

"Go it, Binnski… Stick to it!"

MacTaggart had dropped to third place, and Binns major and Temple were running neck and neck.

The Headmaster, under Mr Russell's guidance, was filming every step of the desperate struggle. The white figures flashed past his lens and breasted the tape with inches between them. The cheers swelled, then died away as the result was announced – Binns major first, Temple second, MacTaggart third.

Raleigh roared again, for they had won first and second places and were now three points ahead. In the wave of excitement that billowed across the field, nobody noticed that Darbishire was missing.

"440 yards – under twelve," called Mr Carter, and Jennings lined up with Venables, Atkinson, Martin-Jones and Rumbelow.

"You're lucky, Venables, having spiked shoes," said Martin-Jones enviously.

Jennings, busily digging footholds with a penknife, remarked: "I'm going to run in my bare feet, if they'll let me. My famous home-made spiked shoes fizzled out into spivish lethal torture, when I put them on."

"Get to your marks," said Mr Carter. "Hurry up, Jennings – we're all waiting."

"I've got to dig holes to get a good start, sir."

"You needn't dig halfway down to Australia. You'll fall into it, if you dig a pit that size."

"Yes, sir. Please sir, may I run in my bare feet?"

"No. For goodness' sake get to your mark – I'm waiting to start the race."

"Yes, sir."

"It's one lap remember, but don't try to sprint the whole way. On your marks… Get set…"

There was a sharp report and the race had started.

Darbishire recovered his breath behind the clump of bushes. His stitch was better, and he felt ready to go on. Although he knew the race was over, wise words of his father's about *Never saying die*, and *Going on to the bitter end*, floated into his mind. No one should say that C E J Darbishire gave up and failed to finish the course.

He ran on, leaving the cover of the bushes as Jennings, with Venables close on his heels, rounded the first bend, eighty yards behind him.

The going was fast and the spectators were cheering with mounting excitement, as the Headmaster seized the ciné camera from its case.

"Quick, Mr Russell," he said, "am I holding it properly?"

"Have a look through the view-finder," replied his instructor. "What can you see?"

"They're just disappearing behind the bushes," said the Headmaster, holding the camera to his eye, and a moment later he exclaimed: "Here they come; they're out on the other side. Venables is running third, Jennings is second and… Who is that boy in front?"

He narrowed his eyes, and then opened them wide in surprise. "Good heavens, it's Darbishire!… Run up, Darbishire, faster, boy, faster."

"Jennings is gaining on him," shouted Mr Russell, as excited as any Form I boy.

"He won't do it," cried the Headmaster. "Darbishire's lead is too great… Run up, Darbishire, run up…you'll win, if you stick to it!"

He hurried across to the finishing tape, and the camera whirred into action. Darbishire winning a race was an event not to be missed!

The runners raced down the final straight and surged past the tape – a breathless Darbishire was in the lead, while Jennings, wearing a puzzled look, finished a yard behind him.

"Darbishire first, Jennings second," exclaimed the Headmaster. "Well run, Darbishire! I didn't think you had it in you." But Darbishire had no breath left to reply.

"It's amazing, Carter," the Headmaster went on, as his assistant approached. "I never thought that boy would beat Jennings."

"He didn't," Mr Carter corrected. "Darbishire wasn't in that race."

"But of course he was in it. He's just won it by a yard. I saw him."

"No, sir. That wasn't Darbishire winning the 440 – that was Darbishire coming in last, in the race before!"

From behind him, the Headmaster heard a sound like a wheezy railway engine.

"*Choof-choof-choof-choof!*" Mr Russell's sense of humour was troubling him again.

17

The Vital Clue

There was an interval for lemonade and buns, which were stacked on trestle tables in front of the pavilion. The boys made short work of this, while the visitors retired to the tea tent, where Mrs Caffey waited upon them with tea and paste sandwiches. Mr Russell politely refused a second cup of tea, and emerged from the tent to find Jennings waiting for him.

"Oh, please, Mr Russell, will you try and take a photo of Darbishire in the egg-and-spoon? You can't count him as being in the last race because they made him a displaced person?"

"I'm afraid I can't, Jennings. Your Headmaster has bought the camera now. He went a hit higher than your bid of three and sevenpence, so I sold it to him."

"Oh, cracko!" Jennings flipped his fingers with delight. "That means we shall be able to have films about all sorts of things now. I wonder if he'll let us use it."

"Not if he wants to keep it in one piece," the salesman replied. He was feeling more light-hearted than he had done for years. He had spent a delightful afternoon in pleasant surroundings – it was all so different from his usual dull routine; and in his wallet was a cheque for ninety-five guineas, signed by M W B Pemberton-Oakes. That ought to please Mr Catchpole! In a sudden burst of generosity, Mr Russell whipped the wallet from his pocket and took out a ten shilling note.

"By the way, that Latin book you've got to pay for – how much is it?"

"Five shillings, I think."

"Well, here's ten. Call it your commission on the sale of the camera; I shouldn't have sold it, if it hadn't been for you."

"Oh, no, really Mr Russell. I couldn't possibly," Jennings protested. "It's awfully decent of you, but I'd rather not – you've done more than enough for me, already."

Nothing could persuade Jennings to accept the present, so Mr Russell shook hands and prepared to leave. He had telephoned for the village taxi, which drove up as he was making a round of goodbyes.

"I'm so glad to have met you," the Headmaster smiled, "and I'm more than pleased with the camera. It's astonishing how many interesting things one sees, which would be lost for ever, were it not for the camera's all-seeing eye. For instance, I happened to be taking a shot of Mr Wilkins drinking a cup of tea outside the tent, when Mr Carter accidentally let the starting-pistol off just behind him; and I now have a permanent photographic record of Mr Wilkins' facial expression as he spilt the cup of tea on his knees. Most diverting. Ha! ha! ha!"

The camera had done much to take the Headmaster's mind off the depressing subject of the burglary, and he was in a jovial mood as he shook hands with his guest.

"Goodbye, Mr Russell," he said as the salesman stepped into the waiting taxi. "And you will remember me to the family next time you see them, won't you?"

"Family? Which family?"

"Mr Jennings, of course. Mr Jennings of Haywards Heath."

Mr Jennings of Haywards Heath! Suddenly something clicked in Mr Russell's mind, and he remembered clearly where his old business acquaintance lived. It was a disturbing memory, and it worried his conscience.

"Oh, yes, Mr Jennings, of course. By the way, Headmaster, I've just remembered something."

"Oh, and what's that?"

"I've just remembered that the Mr Jennings that I know lives at Weston-super-Mare."

The taxi man, anxious to be off, let in the clutch and Mr Russell disappeared down the drive, leaving a puzzled M W B Pemberton-Oakes, Esq. behind him.

"Now, whatever did he mean by that?" he asked himself, and sent Bromwich minor to find Jennings.

They were lining up for the egg-and-spoon race when the message was delivered. Jennings had not entered for this, and he was giving Darbishire some last-minute coaching in the art of egg balancing.

"You're wanted by the Arch-beako," Bromwich minor announced cheerfully. "I don't know what's up, but I should say he's briefing himself for a roof-level attack."

Jennings sensed trouble looming up again and went in search of the Headmaster; he found him staring thoughtfully down the drive.

"Yes, sir?"

"Oh, yes, Jennings – didn't you tell me that Mr Russell was a friend of your family."

"No, he said that, sir – I didn't," Jennings replied. "He told me he thought he might be, but he couldn't be sure."

The Headmaster was mystified. "But if he isn't a family friend, why on earth should he come down here to see you? The school rules are most particular on that point."

"Well, sir – you see, sir, it was like this, sir."

How could he explain? There seemed to be school rules about everything – perhaps about writing for catalogues, and certainly about encouraging salesmen to pay visits. Jennings was wondering where to begin, when Mr Carter suddenly announced the start of the egg-and-spoon race.

"Sir, aren't you going to film the egg-and-spoon, sir?" Jennings said quickly. "It ought to be a jolly decent race for your camera, sir, with everybody dropping their eggs all over the place, sir."

"Don't prevaricate, Jennings. I want to get this business of Mr Russell straightened out. I am at a loss to understand – "

He glanced towards the running-track as the starting-pistol fired, and was so amused by what he saw, that he postponed his awkward questions, and reached for his camera.

The sudden shot had made Atkinson jump; his egg leapt up into the air, and he was making frantic efforts to catch it in his spoon, before it reached the ground.

"Oh, sir, do look at Atkinson, sir," implored Jennings, anxious to keep the Headmaster's attention as far away as possible from questions about unlawful visitors. "And Darbishire, too, sir. He's having an awful lot of trouble with his egg, sir."

Darbishire's expression was a study in earnest concentration, as he battled against overwhelming odds. His egg was wobbling on his spoon and his spectacles were wobbling on his nose. Before he had gone very far, his egg was bouncing about on his spoon like a ping-pong ball.

"By Jove, yes! I mustn't miss this," said Mr Pemberton-Oakes. "Now, let me see: I think I'd better track forwards for a medium close-shot. Stand back, you boys, you're in the way."

The camera whirred and the cheers rose, as the competitors spooned their china eggs unsteadily through the air. Collisions were frequent, and the Headmaster laughed so much that he had difficulty in holding the camera steady.

"Look at Darbishire, sir," laughed Jennings. "He's dropped his egg and his glasses have come off, and now he can't find his glasses to look for his egg!"

The egg-and-spoon race, however, was over all too soon, and again the Headmaster started his investigations. With a heavy heart, Jennings told the story of the Grossman Ciné Camera advertisement; of the letter asking for the catalogue, and the unexpected arrival of the salesman.

Mr Pemberton-Oakes looked stern when Jennings had finished. "This is most disturbing," he said. "It appears that I have been entertaining a false impression of the status of this Mr Russell, and I feel that the matter is of sufficient importance for me to take certain steps."

"Oh, but please, sir, really sir – " Jennings urged desperately. It had been such a splendid afternoon that he could not bear to think of it ending in disaster – the third disaster since breakfast. But the Headmaster's face was forbidding as he continued.

"My considered opinion, therefore, is that if Mr Russell is not a friend of your family – " he paused in thought while his eye travelled round the playing field, noting the happy, excited atmosphere created by seventy-eight boys enjoying themselves to the full. Now, thanks to this Mr Russell and his camera, that happy atmosphere had been captured forever. He turned to his seventy-ninth boy, who stood unhappily before him, and his stern expression relaxed.

"If Mr Russell is not already a friend of your family," he said, "he most certainly deserves to be one in future."

Jennings mumbled his heartfelt thanks and made his escape, as the sound of a car was heard coming up the drive. Mr Pemberton-Oakes stepped forward expecting the new arrival to be General Merridew; and a shadow of annoyance passed over his face as he saw that it was not the General, but Sergeant Hutchinson returning to continue his investigations.

This was the third false alarm in ten minutes. The first time it had been Mr Russell's taxi, then the Dunhambury Float Iron Laundry van had rattled up the drive on its way to collect the hampers from the sanatorium. The Headmaster was becoming anxious; it was essential for him to have a few words with the General before the sports ended, so that he could prepare his important guest for the unpleasant shock which awaited him.

The police car stopped and Sergeant Hutchinson stepped out. "Good afternoon, sir. Will it be all right for us to carry on now, or are we too early?"

"You are rather early," replied the Headmaster. "You see, I'm expecting a distinguished Old Linburian to arrive any moment now. He happens to be the donor of the largest of the stolen cups, and I am afraid he will be most distressed – as indeed we all are – when he hears the sad news." He lowered his voice: "Quite frankly, Sergeant, I'm not at all sure how he'll take it, and I'm most anxious that his first impression will not be of – er – um – "

"You mean he won't like it if he finds the place knee-deep in policemen?"

"Well – I should hesitate to put it quite like that, but I think it might be better if you and your constable, were to – ah – um – "

"Make ourselves scarce. Very good, sir."

Sergeant Hutchinson got back into the car; he drove past the running track and stopped out of sight behind the clump of bushes at the end of the field.

"Coo, look Darbi, there's that policeman again," said Jennings, as the car passed them. "Gosh, I do feel mad about letting him down over that clue I lost."

"And you were going to tell him your suspicions about Old Nightie, too, don't forget."

"Yes, I know. I wonder if he'll think they're important. I don't want him to think I'm making something up, just because I bished up the vital clue."

"Perhaps he'll think you made that up too," suggested Darbishire. "After all, he's only got your word that there ever *was* a button."

"But you can prove that, can't you?"

"Well, I wouldn't like to swear to it, because I hadn't got my glasses on properly, and if you remember I was feeling a bit too much up a gum tree to take things in at the time. My father says that you should never – "

"Oh, you're crackers," Jennings retorted. "Anyway, Mr Carter and Old Wilkie saw it, so that proves it."

"Well, why don't you ask them to go and tell him?"

"Okay, I will."

They trotted across to Mr Carter, who was busy organising the start of the relay. It was the final event and confined to the older boys, and, as the score between the houses stood level, the result would decide the whole contest.

Mr Carter seldom allowed anything to disturb his usual calm, and in the middle of directing eight highly-tensed runners to their stations and listening to Mr Wilkins complaining about the stopwatch, he still had part of one ear available for Jennings' inquiry.

"…and I thought that as I've lost it, sir, you might be willing to tell the policeman, because Darbishire says he might not really believe me, sir. And you know it's true, don't you, sir? – because I had it in my dressing-gown pocket last night when I showed you and Mr Wilkins, and this morning it wasn't there, sir."

Mr Carter brought his mind to bear on the problem, and ignoring the impatience of Mr Wilkins and the feverish excitement of the relay teams, he said: "I can remember your taking the button out of your dressing-gown, but I can't remember your putting it back there. In fact, now I come to think of it, I believe you put it back in the pocket of your pyjama jacket."

"Gosh, yes," Jennings gasped. "Of course I did! I remember now, sir. Golly, what a bish not thinking that before. Thank you a million times, sir." And he dashed away in the direction of the school buildings.

"Here, wait for me," panted Darbishire. "Not so fast! You seem to forget that I've run one half-mile already this afternoon – well, more or less."

Jennings slackened speed. "I'm going to get the button, so's I can give it to the sergeant."

"Well, what's the hurry? Finding the button doesn't catch the thief, does it?"

"No, I know, but it's a clue; and besides, it'll show the sergeant I'm not such a bad detective as everyone makes out. After all, I'm the head of the Linbury Court Detective Agency and I've got my reputation to think about. If Sherlock Holmes lost a button, what would he do?"

"Use a safety-pin."

"Oh, you're bats!" said Jennings. "If he lost a valuable clue, and then someone gave him a clue about where this clue might be – like Mr Carter has – he'd be after it in a flash."

"Well, we'd better get a move on, or we shall miss the relay."

"I was getting a move on, and you stopped me. Come on, let's hurry."

Into the building, up the stairs and along the empty corridors they raced at top speed, until they reached the dormitory. Jennings rushed to his bed and tore back the bedclothes and

18

Perilous Journey

Jennings and Darbishire stood and stared at each other in bewilderment.

"This is crazy," Jennings burst out. "They must be about somewhere, and I know I didn't leave them in the bathroom, so where are they?"

"Perhaps there's been another burglary," suggested Darbishire.

"Oh, don't be so bats. Who'd want to pinch my pyjamas?"

"Old Nightie, of course, so's he could destroy the evidence."

"But he'd only take the button – he wouldn't beetle off with the whole jacket. I suppose I must have dumped it somewhere, when I was getting a move on to go and see Sergeant Hutchinson before breakfast."

Darbishire started searching, in the hope that Jennings had put his pyjamas in somebody else's bed, by mistake.

"That's funny," he exclaimed with a puzzled expression. "Atkinson's had his pyjamas pinched too!"

He rushed to his own bed, and then to Temple's and Venables', and his face was grave as he looked up and propounded his theory: "Somewhere," he announced, "there must be a vast, black-market network of second-hand, stolen pyjamas. There isn't a single pyjam left in the whole dorm!"

Then Jennings remembered. It was Wednesday – when they always had clean pyjamas, and the dirty ones were sent to the laundry.

He sank down on his bed, deep in gloom. If only he had remembered before! Now it was too late, and the clue had vanished forever. His pyjamas would not be back from the laundry for a week, and it was most unlikely that the button would still be in the pocket.

"What super-rotten-sonic luck!" he muttered. Now that the vital clue had really vanished, it seemed even more important than it had done before. He had no notion of the almost impossible task that he had been expecting Sergeant Hutchinson to accomplish – a task which might have included the examination of every sports jacket in Sussex and beyond. To Jennings, a clue was a clue, and any detective worthy of the name should be able to put it to some useful purpose.

Outside on the running track, the starting-pistol sounded for the last time.

"Oh, golly, and we've missed watching the relay," Darbishire said in dismay. They hurried to the window and were in time to see the first pair of runners tearing along the track. Raleigh carried a baton bound with magenta ribbon, and Drake had a similar one in white.

"There they go," shouted Jennings, forgetting his worries in the new excitement. "Old Hippo's beefing it like mad. Run up, Hippo!"

Together they yelled encouragement, though their words were lost in the general uproar that surged up from the field below. R K Stoddington, the Drake House captain, was living up to the zoological nickname, and charged along the course with all his might. He was the largest boy in the school, and although only thirteen and a half, he was already five-feet-nine, and growing rapidly.

The second pair of runners were hopping up and down, marking time at the double, as though they could hardly wait to seize the baton and dash off on the next stage of the race. The Raleigh runner was five yards in the rear, as R K (Hippo) Stoddington thrust the baton into the waiting hand of his colleague. Together they ran a few paces as the exchange was made, and then the Drake House captain sank exhausted on the grass, blowing and snorting like his namesake of the African rivers.

"Go it, Flybow!" yelled Jennings and Darbishire in unison, as Flittonborough major streaked round the field, now ten yards ahead of his Raleigh opponent.

Then came disaster. Flittonborough major dropped the baton in the act of passing it to Wyatt, the third Drake runner, and precious seconds were wasted. Raleigh shot ahead, and the watchers in the dormitory grandstand moaned aloud as their man got off to a bad start, twelve yards behind the vanishing heels of his rival.

The next section of the track was not visible from the dormitory, for a corner of the classroom block jutted out and obscured the view; and Jennings and Darbishire could only wait with growing impatience until the final pair should streak into sight, fifty yards from the finishing tape.

"It's no good," Darbishire muttered. "We shall never make up the distance after a bish like that."

They strained their eyes ahead, and soon the last Raleigh runner flashed into the straight, pursued by Pringle of Drake, only six yards behind.

"Come on Drake!" Jennings yelled. "Go it Pringo!"

He was too far away to see the set expression on the runners' faces; too far, also, to judge whether Pringle was gaining fast enough to sway the result. They watched spellbound now, forgetting even to cheer, while Pringle cut down his rival's lead to inches, then drew level. As they shot past the tape, the cheering on the field rose to a thunderous roar, but the two boys could not make out which side was being acclaimed the winner.

"I think it's Raleigh," Jennings argued. "It looked like a dead-heat from here, but they wouldn't be kicking up all that hoo-hah if nobody had won, would they?"

"We should have stayed out on the field," complained Darbishire. "Now we'll have to wait until – "

"Ssh!" said Jennings.

The cheering died away to a rumble, and Mr Wilkins' voice could be heard, soaring at full volume across the surrounding acres.

"Re-lay result," he boomed. "Drake House is the winner."

"Hooray!" Jennings hurled himself at Darbishire, and they wrestled happily on Temple's bed, until Darbishire's glasses fell off, and the match was abandoned.

"Good old Drake!" they shouted to the empty dormitory, and danced wildly round the room like a nightmare corps de ballet.

Again Mr Wilkins' voice floated in through the window, adding stop-press news to his last announcement.

"Time for the relay – 58.9 seconds… Distance – six inches."

"Six inches," echoed Darbishire. "The man's mad! They had to run more than a hundred yards each, and you couldn't take fifty-eight seconds – "

"No, you ancient relic. He means there were only six inches between the runners, when they finished. If Pringo had been a bit thinner, we might even have lost."

"Well, we didn't anyway. And the next thing is the line-up for the old General – I haven't seen him anywhere, and it's time he got cracking on the – " Darbishire stopped short. That wretched burglary *would* keep cropping up to wither the bloom of everyone's enjoyment.

Jennings hung out of the window. He was overjoyed that Drake had won, but now that the cheering had died away, there was nothing to take his mind off his failure to retrieve the vital clue. Below him, on the playing field, Mr Topliss, Mr Hind and other members of the staff were shepherding the boys in the direction of the pavilion steps, where they were to stand to welcome the General's arrival. The Headmaster was looking at his watch and peering down the drive; it was twenty minutes to five, and there was still no sign of the important visitor.

As Jennings watched the scene, his gaze travelled round and came to rest on the front door of the sanatorium. Suddenly, his eyes sparkled, and he yelled aloud.

"Quick, Darbi, quick. It hasn't gone yet!"

"What hasn't gone?"

"The laundry. The van's still there – come on, we may just do it, if we run."

Jennings pelted down the stairs two at a time, and took the last four in one enormous leap. Darbishire descended by banister rail, and together the two detectives raced out of the building and across the quadrangle. They took no notice of their friends streaming towards the pavilion, and lining up in straight, orderly files in front of the steps.

They arrived, panting and breathless, to find the van still standing outside the cottage. The baskets had all been loaded, and snatches of conversation from the hall suggested that Les Perks, the driver, was arguing with Ivy about a missing sheet.

"Come on," said Jennings. "Let's see if we can find my pyjamas," and he climbed in through the open doors at the back of the van.

"But what about the driver chap? Hadn't we better tell him?"

"Yes, we will when he comes out, but he won't want to hang about all day. We'll get cracking and see if we can find them first."

There were eight large hampers piled up inside the van, and fortunately, they all bore labels of what they contained. *Dormitory* 4 was marked on the basket at the far end nearest the driver's cab, and the boys scrambled over the other hampers to the object of their search. First, they had to lift another hamper, marked *Dormitory* 6 and *Dining-Hall*, from the top of the pile. It was heavy, but they managed to bump it down and stack it behind them.

Jennings fumbled with the straps, and then threw open the lid of the *Dormitory* 4 hamper. On the top was a pile of night clothes. Atkinson's pyjama trousers were dragged out, and beneath them, Jennings could see the distinctive red and white stripe of his own jacket.

"Here it is, Darbi!" he whispered breathlessly, as his fingers fumbled for the pocket, and a moment later he was smiling in triumph and clutching a small brown button.

"Gosh, what a bit of luck, and only just in – " There was a loud bang behind them and the van doors slammed shut. Footsteps scrunched on the gravel, and the next moment someone leapt into the driver's seat and pressed the starter.

"Hey, quick, open the doors!" yelled Jennings, and Darbishire groped his way past the hampers to the rear of the van. It was practically dark inside, now that the doors were shut, and only a gleam of light shone through the little window in the partition which separated them from the driver.

Darbishire reached the rear doors. "I don't know how to open them," he called back, in a worried tone, "and I can't see."

"Oh, gosh, this is awful," Jennings muttered. "The driver doesn't know we're here and he'll be starting off in a – "

It was unnecessary to finish the sentence, for at that moment Leslie Perks let in the clutch, and the van reversed slowly down the little garden path. He was unaware that he had passengers, and the ancient van creaked and rattled so loudly with the engine in low gear, that their shouts for help were inaudible.

They were still jolting in reverse, when the *Dormitory 4* laundry basket toppled from the pile of hampers on which it was balancing and overturned. Jennings was knocked off his feet, and for a moment all was confusion in the darkened interior. Darbishire beat loudly on the rear doors, and Jennings found himself kneeling amongst a jumbled pile of socks, shirts, vests, handkerchiefs and pyjamas that gave little jumps with each jolt of the vehicle.

He put out his hand to steady himself, and in the dim light his fingers touched something unexpectedly solid.

He groped again, and felt rounded contours and jutting handles, and then, scarcely able to believe his senses, he pulled the Merridew Sports Cup from its protective pile of soiled linen.

"Gosh," he gasped. "Darbi – quick, quick!"

"I'm being as quick as I can," replied the dim form of Darbishire, "but I still can't find the handle thing."

Jennings didn't stop to explain. He was convinced now that Old Nightie was the thief – any casual burglar would have taken the cup away with him, but a night watchman who lived on the premises would find it safer to remove it under cover of the laundry van's weekly visit. He had no time to wonder how Old Nightie was going to reclaim his stolen property, for something had to be done at once to stop the van.

Jennings struggled to his feet and peered through the little window of the driver's cab. He could see the man's left hand resting on the steering wheel, and the next moment he saw something that checked his knuckles in the act of rapping on the glass. The driver's jacket was brown, and one of the buttons was missing from his cuff!

Jennings' mind worked at full speed. In two seconds, Old Nightie had left the court without a stain on his character, and his place in the dock was taken by Les Perks, in his brown jacket. In a flash, he recalled the scene some weeks earlier, when he had helped the driver in his quest for Mr Wilkins' laundry, and the man had wandered off into the library.

"No harm in having a look round, is there?" The words came back to him, as he swayed in the semi-darkness of the rickety van. Many details were still obscure, but the main point was plain – the thief was making off with his booty right under the nose of the police. And if something didn't happen soon, the thief would be making off with the two amateur detectives as well.

Holding the cup in one hand, he scrambled along the van to Darbishire, who was still fumbling with the catch on the double doors.

"It's no good, Jen," he gasped. "It must be stuck or something. Whatever shall we do?"

"Here, let me have a go." And Jennings set to work, rattling the catch vigorously.

"The man will be ever so cross when he finds he's got us all mixed up with the dirty washing," said Darbishire, who had no idea of the sensational discovery which his friend had just made. "We shall have to apologise and everything. Oh, gosh, I wonder how far we've gone."

The sanatorium was far behind. The van crossed the quadrangle, passed the main buildings and turned to follow the long line of the drive to the school gates. Before it reached the yew-lined avenue, it skirted one end of the running track and passed in front of the pavilion steps. Here, Perks slowed down, as his path was blocked by lines of boys in bright blazers, patiently waiting for General Merridew to arrive.

The staff were gathered on the pavilion steps, and Mr Hind marched forward and cleared a way through the throng of boys, and signalled the driver to come on. Slowly, the van edged its way through and began to pick up speed again. The next moment, masters, boys and visitors were gaping in stupefied amazement, unable to believe their eyes.

The double doors at the back of the van shot open and Jennings was revealed, clutching the Merridew Sports Cup in one hand, while the other waved wildly in his efforts to prevent himself from falling headlong out of the back. Beside him stood a dishevelled Darbishire, blinking in the sudden light and swaying dangerously as the van gathered speed.

For a moment no one moved. Then Mr Carter seized the megaphone from Bromwich major and shouted to the police car at the far end of the track. Mr Wilkins charged down the drive in the wake of the van, but soon realised that he was unable to run at thirty-five miles per hour, and retired "Corwumphing" with exasperation.

The school seethed with excitement and wonder.

"Gosh, what's happening?"

"Didn't you see?"

"Yes, of course I saw, but what's it all about?"

"Perhaps they're being kidnapped!"

"Don't be so crazy. More likely they took the cup themselves, just for a joke."

"They wouldn't do a thing like that!"

"Well, why are they hoofing off in the van, then?"

"I don't know."

Nobody knew what was happening, though there were plenty of wild guesses. Bins minor was so excited that he hopped up and down, flipping his fingers and barking like a sea-lion. Then he bit his tongue by accident, and became very quiet.

The Headmaster stood quite still and stared at the disappearing figures with an expression of horror and alarm. The next moment, the sleek, black police car was at his side – the constable at the wheel, and Sergeant Hutchinson standing on the offside running-board. Mr Carter flung open the door, pushed the Headmaster inside, and scrambled in after him, as the car streaked off in pursuit.

Round the first bend they overtook Mr Wilkins, glaring down the drive in baffled fury. As they drew level, he leapt on the nearside running-board, and Mr Carter shot his hand out of the rear window and steadied the floundering thirteen-stone-six, with a firm grasp.

"They went that way!" Mr Wilkins shouted, waving his free hand wildly at the drive in front of them.

"Naturally," Mr Carter replied calmly. "There's no other way they could have gone."

The constable accelerated, and round the next bend they sighted the laundry van in the distance, jolting along towards the gates. Jennings and Darbishire were still standing in the back, and as soon as they saw the police car, Jennings waved the Merridew Sports Cup above his head.

"Gosh, look, Darbi, they've got on our trail. Oh, wizzo!"

"Thank goodness," Darbishire sighed with relief. "I don't like this a bit. My father says that – "

What Darbishire's father said was never revealed, for at that moment Leslie Perks caught sight of the police car in his driving mirror. He had been feeling quite sure of himself until then, for he knew nothing of his passengers in the back, and even the shouts of Mr Wilkins had failed to make themselves heard above the noisy engine.

At first, he decided to take no notice; if he were stopped he would plead ignorance of what the hampers contained; but he could not help feeling worried by the purposeful stance of Sergeant Hutchinson on the running-board. Then he glanced over his shoulder through the little window behind him, and caught a brief glimpse of the wide-open doors, and a figure brandishing a silver cup out of the back.

Leslie Perks was not an experienced thief, and this was the first time that he had tried his hand at housebreaking. Immediately, he became flustered, and without stopping to think, he plunged his foot down on the accelerator, in a desperate effort to shake off his pursuers. The old van swayed drunkenly on its creaking springs, and in the back, boys and baskets were tossed about as the vehicle lurched forward protestingly.

"Oh, this is dreadful!" Darbishire's teeth were rattling with the vibration, and he clung to a wobbling pile of baskets for dear life. "Why do these ghastly things always have to pick on me to happen to?" he wanted to know.

The police car was gaining rapidly, as they approached the wrought-iron gates standing open at the end of the drive, and the van plunged on towards the blind corner at reckless speed. Shaking in every nut and bolt and with its engine flat out, it had reached a point barely ten yards from the main road, when a grey Rolls Royce purred quietly in through the main gates and blocked its path.

With screeching brakes the van swerved crazily, mounted the bank, and shuddered to a halt in the hedge; and a moment later, as the police car reached the scene, two figures leapt from the running-boards and rushed up the bank in pursuit.

From the Rolls Royce stepped Lieut.-General Sir Melville Merridew Bart., DSO, MC – purple with rage.

"You – you wretched road hog!" he spluttered in the direction of the laundry van. "What on earth do you think you're doing – hey?"

He caught sight of the Headmaster amongst the figures dashing between drive and hedge, and barked: "Look here, Pemberton-Oakes, what's going on? What's the meaning of – ?"

"One moment, General," the Headmaster broke in, "a state of emergency has arisen. We are trying to catch a burglar."

"Splendid, splendid," retorted the General, who always enjoyed states of emergency. "Anything I can do?"

"Yes, you can hold this for me." The Headmaster thrust a ciné camera into the astonished General's hands, and hurried off into the hedge, to make sure that Jennings and Darbishire had come to no harm.

General Merridew was a man of action. He had no notion of what was going on, but he found himself with a camera in his hands, and a scene of confusion before him. So he put the camera to his eye and pressed the switch.

19

Wednesday Evening Masterpiece

So many things were happening at once that no one, except the General, had a very clear picture of the scene as a whole. Leslie Perks had leapt from his seat when the engine stalled, and dashed back on to the drive in an effort to escape through the main gates; but Mr Wilkins saw him coming, and brought him crashing to the ground with a superb rugger tackle.

Jennings and Darbishire, both badly shaken, scrambled down from the back of the van and assured the anxious Mr Pemberton-Oakes that they were unhurt.

"Yes, sir, thank you, sir, I'm quite all right, sir," gasped Jennings. "Oh, sir, isn't it corking! I mean, isn't it wonderful, sir? We shall be able to have the cup presented after all."

"Never mind about that," replied the Headmaster. "The main thing is that you two impetuous little boys have suffered no ill-effects."

"We haven't suffered very much yet, sir," said Darbishire, expecting to suffer far worse if the Headmaster should take a serious view of their activities. "We tried to get out before it started, sir, but – "

"Coo, look!" said Jennings, suddenly.

Two hampers had been tossed out of the van when it hit the hedge. One of them had scattered a pile of laundry over the drive, and through the broken wickerwork sides of the other could be seen the outlines of the cricket cup, carefully protected by table napkins.

Mr Carter opened the other hampers. The soccer cup was nestling at the bottom of a basket marked *Dormitory* 2, the rugger and gymnastics cups were found amongst the staff laundry and roller-towels, and the swimming and boxing trophies came to light amongst the linen of *Dormitories* 5 *and* 6.

It was too late for the flustered thief to deny all knowledge of what the hampers contained. The fact that he had tried to run away when the van struck the hedge, was a clear indication of guilt, and he offered no further resistance when Mr Wilkins removed his thirteen-stone six and got to his feet.

Sergeant Hutchinson scribbled busily in his notebook, and a few minutes later Perks was escorted to the police car, which left soon afterwards for Dunhambury. After that, Mr Carter drove the van out of the hedge and backed it farther up the drive, where it waited for Sergeant Hutchinson to arrange for its removal.

"Come along, get in," ordered the General, stepping into his Rolls Royce. "It's high time I presented that cup before anyone else tries to make off with it."

The Headmaster sat in front with his guest, and the two boys, with Mr Carter and Mr Wilkins, climbed in the back and nursed the seven trophies.

"I still don't quite see what happened," Jennings queried, as the General pressed the starter. "Why didn't he take the cups away with him, last night?"

"Because this way would have been much safer – if it had worked," Mr Carter replied. "He could use the van only when he was on duty, and if the police had seen him walking through Dunhambury in the middle of the night with a large parcel, he'd certainly have been stopped. I'm afraid we were all a bit off the track in thinking he'd been to the sanatorium first, though."

"You mean he broke into the library to start with, and then took the cups across to the san with him?" Mr Wilkins asked.

"Yes. He'd obviously thought it all out, and when Jennings and Darbishire found him, he was hiding the cups in the baskets, ready to drive them away this afternoon. It's unlikely that anyone would have found them, because if you boys hadn't met him, no one would have known he'd ever been there."

"Wait a moment," put in Mr Wilkins. "Hawkins would have known, wouldn't he?"

"Not last night," said Mr Carter. "You forget the clinker in the boiler. That chap didn't know about Hawkins. It was just good luck for him that he chose the right night."

"And bad luck for him that we did, too," added Jennings.

But there was one point that still puzzled him. How was it that the cups were not discovered when his pyjamas were packed that morning? It puzzled Mr Carter, too. But Leslie Perks could have answered it; for he had counted on Ivy's strict routine of adding the pyjamas to the top of the baskets, and not interfering with the carefully packed linen below.

"All the same," Darbishire argued as the pavilion came into sight, "I bet the police would have found them in time. They'd have searched through the baskets this evening, I expect."

"But by this evening, they wouldn't have been there," Mr Carter reminded him. "I expect he was planning to drive to his house and take the cups out, before going on to the laundry."

The Rolls Royce purred quietly up the drive and stopped in front of the pavilion. The ranks of excited boys straightened as the car approached, and all eyes strained, in the failing light, to see the passengers seated inside. They saw Jennings, pale but triumphant, with Darbishire smiling self-consciously at his side; they saw Mr Wilkins, grimed with dust and wearing his tie knotted beneath his left ear, in the style usually favoured by Binns minor; they saw the Headmaster, trying to look as though nothing out of the ordinary had happened, and General Merridew looking pleased – as a man of action should be – at the successful outcome of the skirmish by the main gates. Then they saw the Merridew Sports Cup in Mr Carter's lap, and seventy-seven boyish throats cheered themselves hoarse.

The Headmaster stepped out of the car and raised his hand for silence. The noise ceased at once, and everyone craned forward eagerly. It was clear that Mr Pemberton-Oakes was about to make an announcement, and the school stood with bated breath to hear the sensational news.

"As we are a few minutes behind schedule," the Headmaster said, "tea will be at six-fifteen this evening, instead of six o'clock."

Not a word about the climax of the most exciting event of the term! Seething with thwarted curiosity, the boys made their way into the lighted pavilion; in baffled silence they listened as General Merridew was introduced, and talked for twenty-five endless minutes about school days being the happiest time of his life.

Late that evening, Mr Carter knocked out his pipe and glanced at the clock on his study mantelpiece. It was time he started off on his nightly tour of the dormitories. The General had gone, after asking for a half-holiday and presenting his cup, which once more occupied the place of honour in the library. This time, however, the white ribbon of Drake was tied round its stand instead of the magenta of Raleigh, and H Higgins,

Jeweller and Silversmith, would soon be engraving the name of the new winner on the trophy's side.

The fame of the Linbury Court Detective Agency had spread round the school during the evening; its health had been drunk in the dining-hall at cocoa-time, and gargled in the dormitories at bedtime. The Headmaster, however, had drunk no healths. He was pleased that the burglar had been caught and the challenge cups returned, but he was distressed at the way in which it had happened.

"You see, Carter," he had explained to his assistant, after lights out, "they might easily have run into danger. However good their intentions were, they had no business to allow their zeal to outrun their discretion in this disturbing manner. Frankly, I am in a quandary. They assure me that their journey in the van was accidental, and was the result of being unable to alight before the vehicle started. Am I to punish them for breaking school rules, or congratulate them on restoring stolen property?"

"I'll have a word with them tomorrow if you like, sir," Mr Carter had promised. "I think perhaps I can guide their interests away from detection, and give them something more suitable to do."

"I wish you would." The Headmaster had sounded relieved. "Perhaps it would be as well if you were to absorb their energies in another chess tournament. Admirable game, chess – there's nothing like it for developing the powers of quiet, thoughtful concentration."

When Mr Carter reached Dormitory 4, he found that Jennings was still awake.

"Hallo, sir," he said, in a loud whisper.

"Aren't you asleep yet, Jennings?"

"No, sir – I'm much too excited. Darbishire is, though, sir. He was just telling me what his father always says about something, and he dropped off in the middle. But I don't feel like going to sleep yet, sir – I want to go on thinking about the burglary and whether Sherlock Holmes would have done what I did... And I've thought of a wizard game we could play next time it rains on a half-holiday, sir – all about detectives, sir."

Mr Carter sighed as he sat down on the bed.

"Oh, Jennings, whatever am I going to make of you? The harder I try to turn you into a quiet and peaceable citizen, the worse you get."

"Sorry, sir."

"This business of playing at detectives has got to stop. I know I thrust Sherlock Holmes at you, but I had no idea it was going to lead to all this. So from now on, no more Linbury Court Detective Agency – understand?"

"Yes, sir."

There was a short pause, broken only by the heavy breathing of the sleepers around them; then Jennings said: "Sir, is Sergeant Hutchinson a detective, sir?"

"No, I don't think so. Not all policemen are detectives; why?"

"Well, I was thinking, sir, if we're not allowed to play detectives, would it be all right if we played ordinary policemen who *aren't* detectives? You see," he hurried on, "Venables, or someone, could be a burglar and Atkinson could be locked in a room like Darbishire and I were – only it'd have to be behind the boot-lockers really – and Darbishire could be the telephone exchange, if we can get a new battery for the Morse buzzer, and I could be a police-sergeant, sir. And then, we could pretend that the tuck-boxes were police cars and laundry vans, and things – "

"And then you'd all rush round the corridors with your arms rotating like roundabouts, and bump into me whenever I turned a corner. Sorry, Jennings – it won't do. Why can't you play something quiet – chess, for instance?"

"Oh, but sir, the Head won't let me. He said it made too much noise the last time I played."

"I think he might stretch a point, if you were really keen"

"Well, all right then, sir," Jennings conceded. "We could bring that in too. We could give Venables, or whoever the burglar was, twenty years in prison, and then we could take it in turns to be warders and go and play chess with the lonely convict, to cheer him up a bit, in his cell – only it'd have to be behind the boot-lockers really, sir…"

For several minutes the eager voice prattled on in the darkness, while Mr Carter sat on the bed and listened to the imaginings of Jennings' mind. Then the prattle became slower, like a gramophone beginning to run down, and finally, it slurred off into sleepy fragments and stopped altogether.

Everything was quiet now; and so much had happened in the last twenty-four hours, that Mr Carter was more than thankful that life was back to normal. From where he sat, the master could see the sanatorium and the silhouetted form of Old Nightie, as he moved, mop in hand, in front of the lighted windows.

When he looked down again, he saw that the principal of the former Linbury Court Detective Agency was fast asleep.

Mr Carter crept quietly from the dormitory and returned to his room. It had been a tiring day and he was quite ready for bed; but one task yet remained to be done. He took a sheet of paper from his desk, and started to work out the details of a long and complicated chess tournament which would occupy Jennings' spare moments for the rest of the term.

"This won't leave much time for Sherlock Holmes," Mr Carter murmured to himself, as he laid down his pen.

Every Wednesday evening, the boys hang up the screen in the common room and the Headmaster fixes the projector. Many of the films are old ones that they have seen before, but this in no way spoils their interest. The boys sit dose up to the screen and watch "Rice Growing in China" and "Plant Life in the Andes" as though they were attending the premiere of the latest Hollywood production. After this, comes a two-minute newsreel of the house boxing finals, or the rugger match against Bracebridge School, and these are watched for the twentieth time with an enthusiasm that never grows stale.

Sometimes, the Headmaster includes the most popular film of all – "Sports Day at Linbury." Everyone has seen it over and over again, but it is such an epic of the screen that the room grows tense with excitement, when the title flickers into view.

"Oh, wizzo, it's the sports again! Super-duper-sonic!" exclaims the audience.

"Look, there's the start of the hundred-yards. Gosh, look at old Hippo, hoofing like a fire engine!"

"Watch out for the next bit – I'm in that. You can just see the back of my heel, if you look in the bottom corner."

Mr Russell was a skilful camera-man. The common room gasps with wonder, as the high- jumpers soar up into the air; then it crouches in mock terror, as the long-jumpers seem to hurl themselves off the screen, right into the lap of the enthralled audience.

Darbishire enjoys the finish of the 440 yards better than anything else. He knows, and everyone knows, what really happened, but he can never suppress his excitement when he sees himself pounding towards the tape – a clear yard in front of Jennings. It is the nearest that Darbishire will ever get to appearing in an Olympic Games newsreel, and he enjoys it to the full.

"It's the egg-and-spoon, in a minute. Do watch Rumbelow – he's got his mouth wide open, as though he's trying to eat it!"

"Yes, I know, and Atkinson looks as though he's playing tennis with his!"

The biggest laugh of the evening is always reserved for Mr Wilkins outside the tea tent. There is a puff of smoke from the starting pistol in the background, and the teacup jumps into the air and lands upside-down on his knee. The Headmaster had intended to cut this scene out, but his assistant would not hear of it; and no one laughs louder than Mr Wilkins, as a coloured close-up of his enraged expression fills the screen, and his lips move in a soundless "*Corwumph!*"

There are glimpses of Mr Carter starting the races; of Bromwich major wearing the megaphone on his head; of the dropped baton in the relay, and the neck-and-neck finish at the tape. But it is after all this has passed, that the film works up to its gripping climax.

The Headmaster always insists that he was photographing the boys lining up before the pavilion steps, and had no intention of including the Dunhambury Float Iron Laundry van in the picture. When the van doors were flung open, he was so surprised that he forgot to switch off the camera for some seconds, and the shot of Jennings and Darbishire's anxious faces as the van recedes, is always hailed with cheers by Binns minor and his colleagues in Form I.

"Ssh!" says the rest of the audience sternly, and leans forward to watch the last act of the drama.

It opens with some confused photography caused by General Merridew's lack of skill as a camera-man. Blurred figures and leaning backgrounds suggest that the General must have been looping the loop when he recorded the pictures, but these distorted fragments soon drop into an ordered pattern. There are brief shots of running feet – then legs, and finally the complete figure of Mr Wilkins flying through the air to bring off the rugger tackle of a lifetime. This part of the film is often

211

commended to the first XV as a perfect demonstration of tackling low.

Then the camera's eye rests on the laundry baskets, and low gasps of wonder fill the common room as Mr Carter brings the sports cup to light.

"What a swizz we didn't know he was taking photos," Darbishire whispers to Jennings in the darkness. "We don't look a bit like detectives – I'm hopping about like a cat on hot bricks, and you look as though you'd just seen the ghost of Hamlet's father. Still, my father says that you can never judge people by appearances and – "

"I should wizard well hope not," Jennings whispers back. "Why, I bet even Sherlock Holmes would look a bit of a chronic ruin, if he'd just been through a frantic hoo-hah like that."

There is a shot of Mr Carter with an armful of trophies and a close-up of Jennings, trying to look unconcerned as he hugs the Merridew Sports Cup to his chest. Then the picture fades into inky blackness; the projector whirrs to a stop, and the lights go on.

There is no doubt, in the mind of the audience, that the film is a masterpiece.

Anthony Buckeridge

According to Jennings

Super-whacko wheeze!

'There you are! How about that for a space-helmet!' cried Jennings triumphantly.

'Jolly good: fits like a glove,' was Darbishire's verdict.

'Attention, all space shipping!' Jennings announced in ringing tones. 'Here comes the one-and-only famous Butch Breakaway, touching down on the moon in his supersonic radio-controlled space-helmet...'

The boys at Linbury Court Preparatory School are eager to speed up the progress of space travel, and none more so than Jennings, whose first task is to find a suitable helmet. But is it really a good idea to take a dome-shaped glass-case, which previously housed a stuffed woodpecker, and place it over his head?

Petrified paintpots!

Jennings and Darbishire's luck is in when they hitch a ride with an international cricketer, and could it be that they've done something right for once when they attempt to apprehend a suspected burglar?

Bat-witted clodpoll!

ANTHONY BUCKERIDGE

JENNINGS' DIARY

Hah-ooh cinosrepus!

'*Selbanev, Nosnikta, Senoj-Nitram,*' said Jennings. 'They're the names of people, I bet you can't guess who!'

'Russian agents?... Zulu tribesmen?... Ancient kings of Egypt?' hazarded Darbishire.

'No, no, no,' Jennings flipped his fingers in delight and danced ungainly ballet steps round the tuck-boxes. 'Oh, wacko! If you can't guess, neither will anybody else, so we can use it for the code.'

Jennings is suffering from beginning-of-term-itis, but things soon return to the normal state of mayhem and confusion when his new diary is made public property! Alarmed at the thought of his most private thoughts being made public, Jennings decides to invent a secret language. Will anyone be able to decode *Selbanev si a llopdolc*?

Drazo Hsivips!

Inspired by a visit to the Natural History Museum, Jennings and Darbishire establish their own collection of ancient relics, but they are not out of trouble for long and when the precious diary goes missing, Jennings finds himself on the wrong side of the law!

Relggowsnroh emoseurg!

ANTHONY BUCKERIDGE

JENNINGS AND DARBISHIRE

Prehistoric clodpoll!

'What did you want to go and make a frantic bish like that for? Rule number nine million and forty-seven: any boy beetling into class with twelve slippery raw fish shall hereby be liable to be detained during Mr Wilkins' pleasure.'

Jennings turns journalist when he receives a printing kit for his birthday, and dubs himself Editor of the *Form Three Times*. Enlisting faithful Darbi as his assistant hack, Jennings sets off to the cove, where a French fishing vessel is moored, for their first story. But when their dreadful French ends in the unwelcome gift of a parcel of raw fish, the worst place they could hide it is in Mr Wilkins' chimney!

Frantic hoo-hah!

Teething troubles fail to deter the tenacious Jennings, and his next scoop involves digging into Mr Wilkins' past – what will he uncover this time?

Super-wacko wheeze!

ANTHONY BUCKERIDGE

JENNINGS GOES TO SCHOOL

Smash-on prang!

'That shepherd's pie we've just had was supersonic muck so it's wizard, but this school jam's ghastly so it's ozard…being a new chap's pretty ozard for a bit, but you'll get used to it when you've been here as long as I have.'

When Jennings arrives at Linbury Court Preparatory School as a new boy, he soon discovers how much he has to learn, especially when the other boys seem to be talking in a different language!

Spivish ozard!

But it is not long before Jennings becomes a celebrity, following an intrepid escape from the school grounds and a riotous attempt to enliven a fire-practice, which leaves Old Wilkie literally climbing the walls! From then on, every time Jennings gives trouble the elbow, a new disaster trips him over. But only one thing really matters to J C T Jennings – his First Eleven debut. When the long-awaited match arrives, Jennings certainly uses his head.

Super-duper breezy!

Anthony Buckeridge

Jennings' Little Hut

Supersonic hoo-hah!

Jennings and Darbishire watched with mounting horror. Earthquakes and landslides seemed to be happening before their eyes. The little hut was heaving like a thing possessed. 'Oh, fish-hooks!' breathed Jennings in dismay. 'He's smashing up the place like a bulldozer!'

The woodland at Linbury Court becomes squatters' territory when Jennings comes up with the idea of building huts out of reeds and branches. Jennings and Darbishire are thrilled with their construction, which even includes a patented prefabricated ventilating shaft, a special irrigation drainage canal and a pontoon suspension bridge!

Gruesome hornswoggler!

But things can only go horribly wrong for Jennings when he is put in charge of Elmer, the treasured goldfish, and even worse when the headmaster pays the squatters a visit. And if Jennings thinks that a game of cricket will be far less trouble, he's going to be knocked for six!

Rotten chizzler!

OTHER TITLES BY ANTHONY BUCKERIDGE AVAILABLE DIRECT FROM HOUSE OF STRATUS

Quantity		£	$(US)	$(CAN)	€
☐	ACCORDING TO JENNINGS	6.99	10.95	16.95	12.00
☐	ESPECIALLY JENNINGS!	6.99	10.95	16.95	12.00
☐	JENNINGS AND DARBISHIRE	6.99	10.95	16.95	12.00
☐	JENNINGS ABOUNDING	6.99	10.95	16.95	12.00
☐	JENNINGS AGAIN!	6.99	10.95	16.95	12.00
☐	JENNINGS AS USUAL	6.99	10.95	16.95	12.00
☐	JENNINGS AT LARGE	6.99	10.95	16.95	12.00
☐	JENNINGS GOES TO SCHOOL	6.99	10.95	16.95	12.00
☐	JENNINGS IN PARTICULAR	6.99	10.95	16.95	12.00
☐	JENNINGS, OF COURSE!	6.99	10.95	16.95	12.00
☐	THE JENNINGS REPORT	6.99	10.95	16.95	12.00

ALL HOUSE OF STRATUS BOOKS ARE AVAILABLE FROM GOOD BOOKSHOPS
OR DIRECT FROM THE PUBLISHER:

Internet: www.houseofstratus.com including synopses and features.

Email: sales@houseofstratus.com
info@houseofstratus.com
(please quote author, title and credit card details.)

OTHER TITLES BY ANTHONY BUCKERIDGE AVAILABLE DIRECT
FROM HOUSE OF STRATUS

Quantity		£	$(US)	$(CAN)	€
	Jennings' Diary	6.99	10.95	16.95	12.00
	Jennings' Little Hut	6.99	10.95	16.95	12.00
	Just Like Jennings	6.99	10.95	16.95	12.00
	Leave it to Jennings	6.99	10.95	16.95	12.00
	Our Friend Jennings	6.99	10.95	16.95	12.00
	Speaking of Jennings	6.99	10.95	16.95	12.00
	Take Jennings, For Instance	6.99	10.95	16.95	12.00
	Thanks to Jennings	6.99	10.95	16.95	12.00
	That's Jennings	6.99	10.95	16.95	12.00
	The Trouble With Jennings	6.99	10.95	16.95	12.00
	Trust Jennings!	6.99	10.95	16.95	12.00
	Typically Jennings	6.99	10.95	16.95	12.00

ALL HOUSE OF STRATUS BOOKS ARE AVAILABLE FROM GOOD BOOKSHOPS
OR DIRECT FROM THE PUBLISHER:

Tel: Order Line
          0800 169 1780 (UK)
          1 800 724 1100 (USA)
          International
          +44 (0) 1845 527700 (UK)
          +01   845 463 1100 (USA)

Fax: +44 (0) 1845 527711 (UK)
          +01   845 463 0018 (USA)
          (please quote author, title and credit card details.)

Send to: House of Stratus Sales Department   House of Stratus Inc.
          Thirsk Industrial Park   2 Neptune Road
          York Road, Thirsk   Poughkeepsie
          North Yorkshire, YO7 3BX   NY 12601
          UK   USA

PAYMENT

Please tick currency you wish to use:

☐ £ (Sterling)   ☐ $ (US)   ☐ $ (CAN)   ☐ € (Euros)

Allow for shipping costs charged per order plus an amount per book as set out in the tables below:

CURRENCY/DESTINATION

	£(Sterling)	$(US)	$(CAN)	€(Euros)
Cost per order				
UK	1.50	2.25	3.50	2.50
Europe	3.00	4.50	6.75	5.00
North America	3.00	3.50	5.25	5.00
Rest of World	3.00	4.50	6.75	5.00
Additional cost per book				
UK	0.50	0.75	1.15	0.85
Europe	1.00	1.50	2.25	1.70
North America	1.00	1.00	1.50	1.70
Rest of World	1.50	2.25	3.50	3.00

PLEASE SEND CHEQUE OR INTERNATIONAL MONEY ORDER
payable to: HOUSE OF STRATUS LTD or HOUSE OF STRATUS INC. or card payment as indicated

STERLING EXAMPLE

Cost of book(s):..................... Example: 3 x books at £6.99 each: £20.97
Cost of order:...................... Example: £1.50 (Delivery to UK address)
Additional cost per book:............... Example: 3 x £0.50: £1.50
Order total including shipping:.......... Example: £23.97

VISA, MASTERCARD, SWITCH, AMEX:

☐ ☐ ☐ ☐ ☐ ☐ ☐ ☐ ☐ ☐ ☐ ☐ ☐ ☐ ☐ ☐ ☐ ☐ ☐ ☐

Issue number (Switch only):

☐ ☐ ☐

Start Date: **Expiry Date:**

☐☐ / ☐☐   ☐☐ / ☐☐

Signature: _____

NAME: _____

ADDRESS: _____

COUNTRY: _____

ZIP/POSTCODE: _____

Please allow 28 days for delivery. Despatch normally within 48 hours.

Prices subject to change without notice.
Please tick box if you do not wish to receive any additional information. ☐

House of Stratus publishes many other titles in this genre; please check our website (**www.houseofstratus.com**) for more details.